W9-DAW-487

FALLING INTO THE
DRAGON'S MOUTH

Falling into the Dragon's Mouth

Holly Thompson

Henry Holt and Company

New York

Henry Holt and Company, LLC
Publishers since 1866
175 Fifth Avenue
New York, New York 10010
mackids.com

Henry Holt® is a registered trademark of Henry Holt and Company, LLC.
Text copyright © 2016 by Holly Thompson
Illustrations copyright © 2016 by Matt Huynh
All rights reserved.

Library of Congress Cataloging-in-Publication Data
Thompson, Holly.
    Falling into the dragon's mouth / Holly Thompson.—First edition.
        pages   cm
    Summary: "In this novel in verse, a resilient American boy deals with
bullying and the challenges of being an outsider that come with living in a
Japanese fishing village"—Provided by publisher.
    ISBN 978-1-62779-134-2 (hardback)—ISBN 978-1-62779-135-9 (e-book)
    [1. Novels in verse.   2. Americans—Japan—Fiction.   3. Bullying—
Fiction.   4. Schools—Fiction.   5. Japan—Fiction.]   I. Title.
    PZ7.5.T45Fal 2016   [Fic]—dc23   2015012291

Our books may be purchased in bulk for promotional, educational, or business
use. Please contact your local bookseller or the Macmillan Corporate and
Premium Sales Department at (800) 221-7945 ext. 5442 or by e-mail at
MacmillanSpecialMarkets@macmillan.com.

Book design by Liz Dresner

First Edition—2016
Printed in the United States of America by R. R. Donnelley & Sons Company,
Harrisonburg, Virginia

10 9 8 7 6 5 4 3 2 1

For Bob, Dexter, and Isabel

What you learn today, you can teach another the next day.

—from *Ki Sayings* by Kōichi Tōhei (1920–2011), founder of Ki Aikido

Chapter 1

SEAT CHANGE: *HAN* SIX

we draw numbers
picking slips of folded paper
from Ōshima-sensei's box
matching them
to a map of desks
to find our *han*—

    the group we'll

    sit with

    clean with

    study with

    for the next

    two months

I hope for at least
one friend

and by *friend*
I don't mean
what I used to mean by *friend*
before I moved to Japan
before I started here
at this school once called
Dragon's Mouth

by *friend* I just mean
anyone who doesn't
punch me
for using the wrong word
kick me
for having an accent
or call me
stinking foreigner

but this time
I get no *friends*
I get
Shunta
Gō
Yuki
Naho
and Mika

Shunta being the one
who hurled a chair
out the classroom
balcony door

Gō being the one
who hit my friend Yōhei
above his left eye
requiring stitches

Naho and Yuki
being the girls
all the other girls
are afraid of

and Mika being the one
who cuts everyone down
with her sword-sharp
words

as we push desks
into position
Mika points
to her seat
beside mine
checks the map
says *no way!*
next to the stinking foreigner?
and they all laugh

she keeps a gap
between her desk
and mine

across from me
Gō slides his desk back
to do the same

kids from all
the other *han*

point
murmur
stare

I expect Ōshima-sensei to help—
        separate my *han* members
        divide them up
        spread them out
        save me

but he frowns
says
I expect no trouble
from han six

he seems to think
I can fend for myself
since I'm a year older
having repeated a grade
when we moved to Japan

      but being a year older
in grade six
in this school
in this out-of-the-way
seaside neighborhood
where hardly anyone
isn't Japanese

      makes me even more different
than I already am
even more the nail
that sticks out
just waiting
to be hammered down

in two periods of science
with Takata-sensei in the lab—
I have ninety minutes to think
on how to survive
nearly two whole months
in *han* six

Yōhei, Shō, Ken, and I
take plant specimens to our station
slice across stems, set them in water
for observing changes day by day

I laugh with Yōhei like he expects me to
write observations like I'm supposed to do
draw diagrams like we're told to

but I feel sick
watching Shunta and Gō
across the room
waving cutter knives
making nicks in the desktop
and dicing an eraser
into smaller
and smaller
pieces

lunch is in the classroom
back with *han* six
eating chicken stuff on rice
salad with cucumbers
and a *mikan* orange

trying to chew
and swallow
surrounded by
Shunta
Gō
Yuki
Naho
and Mika

Naho eats her *mikan* fast
and wants another
so I give her mine
thinking
     maybe I can change her mind
     about foreigners

8

Naho stares at my *mikan*
sitting on her tray

I don't like fruit I explain

but she says *iyada!*—no way!
won't take it
won't touch it
tells Mika to remove it
from her tray

which Mika does
with thumb and finger
then throws it to Shunta
who puts it in his pocket
and says he'll
feed it to his dog

I don't finish my rice
can't finish my rice
knowing my day
will only get worse
because after lunch is

cleaning

upstairs in the music room
no teacher
just me with
Shunta
Gō
Yuki
Naho
and Mika

Chapter 2

CLEANING

we're supposed to
move desks aside
sweep the floor clean
then put the desks back

I take a broom
to get started
but Shunta yanks it
right from my hands

he shoves me
and forces me
and only me
to use the dustpan

here, boy, here they say
Shunta, Gō
Yuki, Naho, and Mika
again and again

making me
and only me
sweep up
tiny piles of dust

I sweep fast with
one quick flick
of the dust broom
while watching my back

when they quit
and sit on desks
I quit and sit on a desk

but they yell
Jason! Move it!
to make me sweep up more

I glare at them
and don't move
until Gō approaches

then I hop off, start putting
desks back into position
like we're supposed to

always careful
to keep
a desk
        or chair
between me
and Gō

later, walking home
Yōhei, Shō, and Ken
try to encourage me
share strategies

tell me not to
        meet their eyes
        listen to insults
        act scared

tell me to
        laugh at their jokes
        keep out of their way
        and never fight back

I can't I say

you have to they argue
it's the only way

but I've watched Gō and Shunta
and I know they're just waiting
to push me too far

at home I kick off my shoes
drop my backpack
head up to my room, planning
to lie down on my top bunk

but in ~~my~~ our room
my sister Cora's playing teacher
with her second-grade friend
  their stuffed animals
  lined up in rows
  all over the *tatami*
  so I can barely
  walk in the door

I holler at her
kick a stuffed moose
step on a squirrel
and slam the door

in the living room
I flop down on the couch
my face smooshed
against cushions
and lie there immobile

till Mom shouts from the kitchen
where she's grading papers
that it's time to do homework
and put on my aikido *gi*
and, by the way . . .

she needs to talk to me
about taking care of Cora
on Wednesdays
since she's been offered
two more classes to teach

iyada—no way!
I yell into the cushion
nasty
just like Naho said it to me

but suddenly Mom's hands
are hauling me up by one arm

> *Jason Parker* she says
> *we don't talk like that in this house*
> *so go clean up the genkan*
> *then start your homework*

I move the stupid shoes
out of the way
and sweep the stupid *genkan*
then line up the shoes
with toes facing out

all proper
in case some neighbor
stops by

except

I pair the shoes
     right shoe on left
     and left shoe on right

hah!

Chapter 3

CENTERING

it's dusk when I leave for the dojo
switch on my bicycle light
and coast downhill toward the temple
where I cross the main road
cut into an alley, cross the bridge
and ride the lane that follows the river

there you can hear the slap
and splash of fish jumping
so I sometimes stop and wait
straining to see fish in the dark
but today I'm late and pedal past
to the house that's really a dojo

I started aikido
after moving here
in third grade
after I learned
that soccer here
is all afternoon
every Saturday
every month
all year long

with kids like Shunta and Gō
and a coach who did charades
to explain things to me
then tried simple English
and laughed hilariously
like it's the funniest thing in the world
        to speak English

the dojo is different

at the dojo
you start with a white belt
no matter who you are
girl or boy

you do the moves
with everyone else
no matter your age
or size or rank

you take tests
to advance levels
no matter your age
or size or rank

you get respect
you give respect
no matter your age
or size or rank

I was white
then green
then yellow belt
now I'm orange
trying for blue

at the dojo
you bow to enter
and on the mats
you kneel, you meditate
you hold your one-point center
even when Yamada-sensei
pushes your forehead to test you

you chant, you stretch
you roll
  across
    the mats
      forward
    and back
you bow to your opponent
you practice holds and moves
you take your opponent's energy
and turn it to overcome him
  or her

and what matters most
through every move and fall
is you keep firm
you stay in control
you hold your center

in aikido
we practice protecting
we imagine attackers
we use mind and body together
our *ki* energy
to keep calm
perform our best
so we can dare to face
an enemy of millions

but today I picture real attackers

so while entering and turning
and receiving strikes
I'm thinking of
Shunta
Gō
Yuki
Naho
and Mika

I focus hard
make no mistakes
calm and action
as one

Chapter 4

ENGLISH GROUP

being away
from the Dragon's Mouth
and *han* six
for a total of
sixty-five weekend hours
makes Monday morning
back at school
the worst—

    Mika stabbing me with her words
    Gō slamming me every time I stand
    Yuki hitting the back of my head
    whenever I make a mistake and
    Shunta and Naho egging them on

all day long Ōshima-sensei
seems blind to my situation
just yelling about noise
way too much noise

so at the final bell I race
from classroom to school gate
to our car waiting uphill
for Cora and me

I feel like telling Mom
step on it
like we're in
a getaway car

even though
we're just driving
the usual route
to English group

English group
is kids like us—
transplants
or *hāfu* mixes
or Japanese returnees
who lived abroad
a long time

a whole group
of English speakers
from different Japanese schools
who meet once a week
in a public hall in Yokohama
to keep up our English—
not just speaking, but also
      reading
      writing
      thinking
      researching
      presenting

we're divided into olders and youngers
and in the olders we're

Will—mom English, dad Japanese

Nenita—mom Filipino, dad Japanese

Erika—mom Japanese, dad Japanese-American

Trina—mom Chinese-Singaporean, dad Japanese

Ami—mom Japanese, dad Ghanaian-Canadian

me, Jason or "J"—mom Polish/Italian-American
dad Dutch/English-American

today Trina's mom is teaching
the olders and youngers together
a new unit on economics
and we're learning about scarcity
which we get when she tricks us
into thinking there are many bags
of popcorn on the table—*help yourselves!*

but the popcorn runs out
when only a few have had any
because it turns out most bags
contain only crumpled paper
so Ami's sister starts bawling
then Trina's mom asks us how
to solve the problem of limited supply

we suggest sharing the popcorn
but the youngers Ethan and Sophie
already opened their bags and ate half
which leads to a lesson on allocation
and resources and choice and then
we break into olders and youngers
for discussions and exercises

we have to come up with
examples of things
in limited supply
and think of a way
to allocate that good
or resource

Will, Nenita, Trina
Ami, and I list
      water
      time
      manga in English
      money for fun stuff
      unicycles at school
      electricity

then we crack up
when Erika who loves fashion
and spends her allowance
on shoes says *shoe closets!*

we laugh and joke
and no one
whacks anyone
on the head

Chapter 5

FIRE

on Wednesday
the first Wednesday
for watching my sister Cora
the wind blows wild—

>   leaves scrape the street
>   shutters bang
>   and a Styrofoam box trips past
>   like it's out for a walk

bōken—an adventure
Cora says for the fifth time
as she unlocks her bike

I nod like I have a plan
but I don't

the wind blows so hard
the air tastes of salt
the temple bell rings too loud
and the streetcar horn blasts too close
like the train has left the seaside tracks
to climb right up to our neighborhood
high on the hill

I don't think you have an adventure planned
I don't think you meant it
Cora says

and for that I take off
before she's ready
flying downhill
ahead of her yells—

Jason! Wai . . .
half-eaten by the wind

I skirt the park
            and coast down
                        weaving in and out
                                    back lanes
                        and alleys

keeping Cora

                                    just in sight
not slowing till we reach
the flats where the streetcar
            runs
            down
            the
            center
            of
            the
            road
and the sea wind blasts
            from breaks
between buildings

I stop
and Cora catches up
whining between breaths

about how fast I went
about how this is so not an adventure
about how I promised her an adventure every Wednesday
  if she'd go along with the plan of me watching her
  so Mom can teach extra classes
  so we'll have enough money
  for me to switch to international school

and I'm about to say
forget it, let's go home
but just then a gust
brings us the scent
of grilled chicken
and I think

  hey!
  grilled chicken
  can be an adventure

this way
I say
and we cut through an alley

to a street with
greengrocers
fish shops
sweet shops
and a tiny meat shop
where the owner and his wife
grill *yakitori*—
skewers of chicken
on charcoal fires

they're friendly
not like some people
in this part of town
who talk too polite
or stare at us
with cold eyes
for being different

irasshaimase!
the butcher and his wife call out
what'll you have today—liver?
and I laugh, liking that they know
what I don't like

they lean forward over the counter
is she your sister? and when I nod
the butcher's wife says
kawaī!—cute!
like a doll!

which Cora hates
but she smiles
plastic-like
and nod-bows

two skewers with scallions I say

and for the young lady? the butcher asks

we'll share I say because
I don't have money for more

he dips the skewers
into a bin of sauce
and sets them on the grill

my mouth
waters
as we wait

where are your friends?
the butcher asks
because sometimes I come
with Yōhei and Shō

juku I say—cram school

not you? he asks
and I groan because
the last thing I want
after school
is more school

already I have
English group
once a week
Japanese tutor
twice a week
plus aikido
twice a week
and now Cora
once a week

the butcher hands over
not two but three skewers
sābisu he says—service
meaning one is free

I hand two to Cora
keep one
and she whispers
we'll share

the salty-sweet sauce
on hot grilled meat
is better than perfect
and I eat mine too fast

then stand there
nearly drooling
waiting for Cora to finish
her half of the extra skewer

as a customer approaches
the butcher starts his greeting
but just then a siren
            splits
                        the air

Cora drops the skewers
            and climbs me like a tree

the customer grabs my arm
            and holds on tight

the butcher sheds his apron
            and races up the street

by the third siren
I can set Cora down
the customer lets go
and the butcher's wife collects
the apron and dropped skewers

fire! she says above the siren

and in this wind! she adds
        eyeing dust and leaves
                plastic bits and paper
        flying through the air

come on! I say to Cora
even though the butcher's wife is
dipping new skewers for Cora

let's go! I say
even though seconds ago
I wanted more

as we pedal off
a car flies past
two workers
race from a side alley
a man in a suit
leaps onto a bicycle

from all sides
men head to the fire station
and rush to a fire truck
where the butcher
now sits in full
firefighting gear

the siren wails
the truck leaves
bells clang
more sirens sound
more bells clang
and shopkeepers
customers, students
even tourists just off the streetcar
stand still as snapshots

and in this wind . . .

Chapter 6

SANDAL

on our bicycles
we follow the noise
and all at once
we smell
then see

    black smoke
    rising

where the fire trucks turn
where the lane meets the river
we stop because upriver a rooftop burns
     flames leaping
     clawing, snapping
     at neighboring homes

fire and rescue trucks
ambulances, police cars
cram every bit of road
or driveway or bridge
and jets of water
stream from hoses

then

sugei nā—cool!
says a voice I know too well
Shunta Mori
who rules *han* six
straddling his bike, his pride
all hand-painted with
lightning bolts and stripes

Yuki's uncle's house is right
behind the fish shop Shunta says

     Yuki
     who knocks me on the head
     when I give the wrong answer
     in class

does she live there? I say

no, idiot, I said it's her uncle's house

I don't bother to argue
I don't bother to say
     that Yōhei lives with his parents
        and grandparents
     that Shō's aunt lives with his family

because what I have learned
in one week with *han* six is that
     Shunta is always right

let's go closer Shunta says

no, it's too dangerous I say
then immediately regret it
because as usual my words
don't come out quite right

what I wanted to say was
 we'd be in the way
 wind could spread this fire fast
 we have a good view where we are now

but in Japanese
my words always sound
too slow
too formal
too adult
or too young

for once Shunta
gives me a break and
just watches the flames
darting in all directions

then he shouts
the next one's burning, too!
and it is

ash and embers fill the air
people pass buckets
from the river to houses
others point hoses
to douse sheds and fences
rooftops and trees

the wind whips—
spray and smoke
sting our eyes
and I'm thinking
what to say to Shunta
so we can just leave

but then a voice says
bōya! oi, bōya!—
boy! hey, boy!

and an old man shuffles over
one hand on a cane
the other clutching
something under his arm

Shunta glares at him
turns back to the fire
the man comes closer
with his eyes on mine

he speaks but
sirens
people's cries
Cora's whines
blasts from hoses
the roar of the wind
take the man's words and
                  send
                        them
                                  sailing

the man shuffles closer
mumbles something
and nudges my arm
with a plastic . . . garden sandal?

Shunta jerks his head
let's go! come on!
as if I'm supposed to
follow, pronto

I don't, and when the man
sandal-taps my arm again
Shunta leans over
bats it down, and says
> *get away with that filthy thing!*
the man catches it
stumbles backward
tucks it under his arm
and moves away

then we all turn to watch the fire
hear the house groan
and see one side collapse
in huge billows of smoke

but Cora slides closer to me
signaling with her eyes
toward the mumbling man
so I shift toward him
he totters toward me, and I hear
police . . . fire . . .
and this time I accept the sandal

baka—jerk! Shunta says
mounts his bike, spits
and rides off a ways

I ignore him
bend toward the man and say
something to do with the fire?

a guy . . . running the old man says
and now I catch scraps of sentences—
motorbike . . . house . . . front . . . this dropped

where? Cora says

yellow house . . .
he slurs and waves toward
a distant two-story house

Shunta returns
yanks my arm
let's go! he says *now!*

so I hook the sandal
over my handlebar
nod at the man

and to Cora
say *come on!*
then follow Shunta

wait, J!
I hear
but I don't turn

because with Shunta
I have to pretend
I just don't care

Shunta leads us downriver
across a bridge and up the other bank
to a small park of tilted pine trees
from where across the water we see
      smoking beams and rubble
      charred dressers
      and scraps of drenched clothing
      like street litter after rain

a few flames flicker and leap
onto an adjacent roof
then the fire is doused leaving
only rising steam and smoke

we hear crying
see a cluster of people
gathered around a woman weeping
and a man covering his face

Yuki's mother and her uncle Shunta says
then swears and spits
her uncle's whole house—just gone

Cora touches the sandal
gives me a sly look
and I nod, barely
so Shunta can't see
and say *we have to go*

Shunta sneers
you taking that sandal?
that man's a fool!
and lets go a torrent of words
that makes Cora's eyes bulge

I duck when Shunta tries
a parting punch
that only barely
grazes my arm because
I move but hold

        my center

Chapter 7

POLICE BOX

we cross the river downstream
and pass the house we think
might be the old man's
where a woman now stands
in front, hands on hips
staring toward the fire

we ride the riverside path
to the road that leads to the beach
and the big intersection
near where the police "box"
sits squeezed between
the post office and a flower shop

inside
the office has
a small counter
a few folding chairs
posters of those same-old
creepy faces of wanted people
and an officer who appears from
a tiny back office

the last name on his name tag
I can read 中里—Nakazato

I set the sandal on the counter

     mistake!

what's this? the officer scoffs
then brushes off the counter
lifts the sandal with one finger
and places a tissue beneath

it's a sandal Cora says
I give her a silencing look
something to do with the fire I add
but Nakazato doesn't flinch

an old man gave it to us I explain
he saw a man running from the fire area
and that man rode a motorbike
in front of the old man's house . . .
and motorbike man dropped this sandal
we think

my Japanese sounds dumb so I add
somewhere there is a man
        on a motorbike with
        one sandal

Nakazato sighs
takes up a pen
so, the old man's name?

Cora and I look at each other
we don't know I say
we can go back to check Cora offers
Nakazato taps his pen

or if you have a map I say
I might be able to show you
and he stands and points
to a huge map tacked to the wall

I run my finger over
neighborhoods, block numbers
tiny *kanji* character names
for each household or business
the main road, the river, bridges
which I count up from the fire station
to the fish shop and the house on fire
then I follow houses downriver
and three houses below another bridge
where the lane narrows to a path . . .

this house I say, and it's marked
　　竹村
　　　Takemura
a simple name I can read

an old man lives there Cora says
his words are hard to understand
and he uses a . . . a stick—
she gestures and limps to show a cane

Nakazato jots down notes
anything else? he asks

I wish we had something else
but we don't

he writes down
> our names
> our address
> home phone number
> cell phone numbers
and gives us
> the police box number

please I say
please find that one-sandal man

and we leave

outside the police box
the five o'clock chimes ring

the groceries! I say
Mom's list and her money
still sit in my shirt pocket
and by now we're supposed to be home
chopping vegetables and starting rice

I try to swear gangster style
like Shunta in Japanese
but Cora just laughs

and for that
I take off again
before she's ready

hah!

Chapter 8

BALANCE AND PERSPECTIVE

the next day the fire
is the talk of the school
han six is distracted
and Yuki is silent
never once
whacking me on the head

without *han* six moving my desk
or making marks on my papers
I can even hand in work early
and place it on the pile of papers
weighted by a bronze dragon
that's been in this classroom
twenty years, so they say

the subject of the fire
comes up again and again
so finally Ōshima-sensei says
to write a reflective essay
or make a newspaper page
or sketch pictures of the fire
or do anything else to reflect

so I draw
the house and flames far upriver
and in the foreground, huge
      a single plastic
      garden sandal

Shunta snorts when he sees it
makes loud fun of it
and I expect the usual
bruising punch to my arm

I try to protect myself
find and hold my center
but the blow comes
      from behind—Gō

            my head rings

I want to punch back
but Shō and Yōhei always say
don't!
it will get worse if you do
just hold on until next seat change

but seat change
is seven weeks away
seat change is not
until the end of November

my head throbs
but I pretend to laugh along
with Shunta and his gang
all crowded over my desk
poking fun at my drawing

my opponents
my attackers

too close

I want it to be five o'clock
I want to be at the dojo

chanting
stretching my neck
                bending my wrists
        rolling over the mats
                forward and back
                        and falling, dropping
                flipping, being flipped
        the slip, slip
                of feet on the *tatami*
with Yamada-sensei's voice
guiding us through moves
to evade strikes
to turn opponents
and get into safe places

but Shunta and Gō breathe
salty lunch smells on me
and start to scribble
right on my sketch

I know better than to act
as if I care

then I get an idea
and say

why yes, a dirty sandal
probably just trash

in a stiff, adult voice

yet this object
gives the painting
balance and perspective
foreground and background

imitating, more or less
the words of our art teacher

and it works—
they snort-laugh
and back away
just enough for me to stand
roll my sketch
have a look at
and pretend interest in
whatever the others drew

     Shunta's mass of licking flames
     Naho's eyeball with reflected flames
     Gō's scratches he calls smoke
     Mika's manga that she hides
          when she sees me looking

my head hurts
from Gō's smack
and I hate
Mika's glare
but I did it
     I turned the opponent's energy
     I controlled the opponent's center

Chapter 9

SATOMI HAS LONG HAIR

Satomi has long hair
that hangs past her waist
and flips over her chair back
and slips through her fingers
as she thinks on an answer

her seat lies behind Shunta's
facing away from me
so that my view past Shunta
just over his left shoulder
is Satomi's hair

I stare
and stare
at this long hair
that falls down her back

that is sometimes in braids
but more often in a ponytail
that she does and redoes
flicking that hair
up off her neck
and lifting it
to feed it
and pull it
through an elastic

then her fingers continue
running through strands
playing the strands
below the elastic band
as she thinks
on a math problem

but if I stare too long
at Satomi's hair
and Shunta sees my attention
drifting from an equation

he

                POUNDS

his fist
on my desk
to make me jump

this Monday
instead of pounding
Shunta follows my stare
to Satomi's hair
and before I can
catch my center
he

smacks

my face

so that my lip splits
and bleeds
onto my math paper
and Mika stands
grossed out
and Naho stares
and Yuki yells at me
to get a tissue
and Gō just waits
to see what Shunta
will do next

it's Yōhei
who taps me from behind
to hand me a tissue

and finally
Ōshima-sensei gets up
from his desk

and strolls over
to see what the noise
is all about

I have an ice pack on my mouth
when Mom and Cora pick me up
for English group, and my lip
is so swollen I can hardly talk

what happened?! Mom asks

I fell I say

and Mom says flatly *you fell*

and Cora says flatly *onto your lip*

and Mom says
but not your nose

and Mom and Cora trade looks
and Cora says *right*

I stare out the window
angry at myself
vowing never again to be
caught

off-center

at English group
they see my lip right away
and the moms and Ami's dad
are all *poor thing!*
but I act like it's nothing

we're doing consumers and producers
and preparing for a marketplace
with the olders as producers
deciding prices of goods like

     handkerchiefs

     pencils

     cell phone straps

     erasers

     toothbrushes

     and stickers

for the youngers

I have to keep icing my lip
and finally Ami looks up
from a price tag and whispers
who hit you?

and when I don't answer
Will asks *some jerk?*

and I nod, knowing
they know what it's like

why? Trina asks
did something happen?

*no, nothing happened
just a jerk being a jerk* I say

without adding that I was
staring at Satomi's hair

in the marketplace
the youngers do the shopping
but they're not so good with money
and don't quite get our sales promotions

Best price guarantee! Today ONLY!
20% off last week's price!
Buy one get the second half price!
Buy two pencils and win a free eraser!
Buy three pencils and get the fourth one free!
Best handkerchiefs for folding into rockets!
Stickers—even your dog will be impressed!
Toothbrushes! Arashi band's brand!

except Cora and Evan
who take the longest to decide
calculating on scrap paper
and purchasing the most goods

at least it diverts my attention
completely

from my lip
from *han* six

Chapter 10

ONE-SANDAL MAN

the next day
I'm sitting at the kitchen table
with Yūsuke, my tutor
a college student
from the university
where my dad teaches

Yūsuke who lived in New York
so he can explain things
to me in English
when I'm lost in Japanese

which is
like
all the time

we're going over readings
for *kanji*
such as *ken*—権—right, authority
 which has five different readings
 and 242 compounds
 too many of which
 Yūsuke seems to find
 endlessly fascinating
 and most of which
 I do not
 but thankfully
 only eight of which
 I have to memorize
 for a test at school
 this week

when the phone rings

I can tell Mom's talking with
someone she doesn't know well
with her voice high-pitched and polite
stumbling over formal Japanese

but then
she brings the phone over to me

excuse me
she says to Yūsuke

then to me
> *it seems a policeman*
> *wants to talk to you*

I recognize the voice, Nakazato-san
the officer from the police box

we talked to the old man he says
who has Parkinson's disease, by the way
that's why his speech is difficult to understand
anyway, he gave a description
of the man on the motorbike

he did? I say

yes the officer says
and we found two people
who'd seen a man
with one sandal
riding a motorbike—
they gave us details of the bike
and from the descriptions
we narrowed down possibilities
asked more questions
and found the man
who set the fire

you did? I say
who?

but the officer won't say
and adds something I don't quite get
to explain why he can't say

then he says
you know
Takemura-san tried to tell others
about the sandal—
> *his daughter*
> *the neighbors*
> *the boy you were with*
but no one listened to him
only you and your sister
truly listened

the officer thanks me
and reminds me
to thank Cora, too

I go upstairs
to find Cora
and she's got her stuffed animals
doing a sports festival
all over our room
            the oval track
            made with a circle of blocks
            animals picnicking on handkerchiefs
            other animals propping up paper score sheets
            for the white team and the red team

but instead of yelling at her
like I usually do
when she does this to *our* room
I tell her what the officer said

sugoi! she says *wow!*
we helped solve a crime!

downstairs I ask my mother and Yūsuke
what's Parkinson's disease?

and Yūsuke starts jabbing at
his electronic dictionary
as my mother brings her laptop
and a medical dictionary
and we spend the rest
of my tutoring session
on words like

      neurological

      symptom

      tremor

      balance

and Yūsuke thinks
it's a perfect opportunity
for me to study compounds
using the *kanji*
for brain—*nō*—脳

um, no!

that night Cora and I
whisper back and forth
in our bunks
who? we want to know
who would set fire
to a fish-shop owner's house?

Cora puts on her headlamp
and we make a list:

    a vegetarian
    a fish (Cora says this)
    another fish-shop owner
    a robber
    the fish-shop owner if he wanted a new house
    someone who got food poisoning from the shop

then Cora says *I bet it was that woman*

who? I say

the one on the wanted posters at the police box

and I laugh—*I'm sure she doesn't live around here!*

well, she could—how do you know?

we run out of ideas
and soon Cora is asleep
but I lie awake
listening to the *rin rin rin*
of the bell cricket
that Yūsuke gave me
and that we moved
to the balcony
because it's so loud

I lie there trying to picture
a man in garden sandals
setting fire to a house
in broad daylight

and I think
that was
crazy obvious

like
did he hope
to be caught?

Chapter 11

SLAPS

then on Wednesday
I learn who

Shunta spreads the news
that it was
the fish-shop owner's
youngest son
Yuki's cousin
who set the fire
angry that his father
wouldn't lend him
money to cover his debts
to a pachinko parlor owner

again
a whole day passes
without Yuki smacking me

a whole day when Yuki looks
not fierce but ready
to cry

Shunta milks it
tells of other times that son
was in trouble
> drinking
> starting fights
> stealing

he says that
people say trouble
runs in that family
like a bad gene

all day long Yuki
trembles and fumes
a volcano

> ready to erupt

then last period
when Shunta makes
one more
stupid wisecrack
about pachinko balls

Yuki stands
throws her chair
right at Shunta
then Shunta throws
his chair back
and we all duck
and move away
and the teacher hollers
and shoves them both
into the hall

we right the chairs
and sit still and jittery
in the classroom
as the teacher yells
and once
then twice
slaps

in Massachusetts
at my old school
some parents wanted
a no-touch rule—
  no hugging
  no holding hands
  no wrestling or poking
  no hitting

a rule that some teachers refused
and most parents ridiculed
as out of place
in elementary school

but inside the Dragon's Mouth
I'd vote in a minute
for that no-touch rule
or at least a no-hit rule

some parents here say
words are not always enough
and even Yōhei, Shō, and Ken say
sometimes a teacher needs to slap

  but I think *really?*

Chapter 12

GYŌZA

after school
I peel away from Shō and Ken
and walk the opposite way
to the after-school center
just up the street
from our school

on Wednesdays second graders
are let out after lunch recess
but sixth graders have school till three thirty
so Cora waits for me there
now that Mom has afternoon
university classes

the after-school center is really just a house
but a house with empty rooms
and some toys lying on open floors
or stacked against beat-up walls

two women who work there
stay mostly in an office
like a closet with a window
from where they watch the kids

the first time we visited, Mom said
you don't play with the kids?

oh, no they said *it's very free here!*
children can do what they want!

no games, crafts, or activities? Mom asked

oh, we do crafts twice each term
we send notices to the school
but the rest of the time they can play—
it's very free!

free
is a word
that we've learned
has a different meaning
in English than
in Japanese

in Japanese
free seems to mean
what Mom calls

     unchecked mayhem

when I arrive at the after-school center
Cora is waiting in the entryway
with her shoes on before
I've even signed her out

she's quiet till we reach the hill
then she says *don't tell Mom*

tell Mom what? I ask

that I hate the kids there! she says
then adds *they call me gyōza*

gyōza?—dumpling?
I laugh
why gyōza?

her eyes start tearing
as she holds out her arm
pointing at the veins

I'm like gyōza—
they can see through
my skin to the stuff inside

I tell her
at least it's a name
of something that tastes good
and that they're just not used
to different types of skin

I tell her
we'll have our adventure
in the park across the town line
the one past the water tower
with the good swings

I tell her
we'll take cardboard for sliding
cardboard boxes that will
fly on the dry grass
just like sleds

and Cora wipes her arm
across her eyes

okay she says

we walk to the park on the hill
beyond the water tower
with a folded
cardboard box each

and we run up and slide down
the wide brown grassy hill
until our hair is
wet from sweat

then after a while Cora makes a friend
and they slide together
then go off to play house
under a tree

and I lie back on the cardboard
stare at the veins
on the insides of my arms
and laugh

I never thought of us
as *gyōza*

Chapter 13

YAKITORI

Friday is the one afternoon
when Yōhei, Shō, Ken, and I
are all free, so we play soccer
two on two, in the small park
near our house

      until they leave for *juku*

where they study more math
more Japanese, more science
to prepare for entrance exams
for private middle schools
the kind connected to high schools
so they won't have to take entrance exams

      again in three years

why aren't you in juku?
even they ask me
even though they know I study
in an English group
once a week
and my tutor comes
twice a week

what they mean is
why don't I go to cram school
so I can test into a private school
so I can avoid going
to the local middle school
where people like
Shunta, Yuki, and Gō will rule
together with other thugs
from all three elementary schools
that feed into our middle school

I haven't told them
that I've already applied
to an international school
that I've already been accepted
and could start right now

I don't want to tell them
that the only problem now
is money

which is why
Mom is teaching extra classes
and why she's not home on Wednesdays
when Cora's grade lets out early
and why she's trying to get a full-time job
like Dad at a university
and why she goes on interviews
and fills out applications
and tries to publish papers
and speak at conferences
and why I'm learning to cook
and buy groceries
and take care of Cora

I don't want to get into this
with Yōhei, Shō, and Ken
so I tell them

> *I'm studying with my tutor*
> *but we just don't know*
> *which schools I'll apply to yet*
> *since my Japanese is weak*

they shrug
and don't ask more questions
about schools

just
who's on whose side
for two-on-two soccer

after barely a game
they all have to leave
so I go home, wash up
and head out again, still with
forty minutes till five o'clock chimes

I ride my bike downhill
in and out of back lanes
to the butcher shop
and order four skewers—
chicken with scallions

to go I say

I wait while they grill the skewers
and when they hand me an extra
and say *sābisu*
I ask them to add that
to the bag, too

I hang the bag from my handlebar
ride to the main road
then the side lane
and park my bicycle
along the riverside path
where the motorbike
must have been left
and the sandal
must have been dropped

I take the bag to the gate
and ring the bell

when no one answers
I ring again
then that slurry voice
comes over the intercom

it's me, Jason, the boy
you gave the sandal to
during the fire I say

ah! the voice says
dōzo!—come in

I push at the gate
the front door opens
and he stands there

I bow, hold out the bag—
I brought some yakitori

and suddenly I think
this was a mistake
because he's scowling

and maybe he can't
chew it
or swallow it
or digest it—

can you eat it?

yakitori? he says
sure! come in!

so I follow his
flapping hand
and step up to the
entryway

and into
Takemura-san's world

Chapter 14

BRAIN LEAP

after my tutor session
after Yūsuke has left
after dinner
in our room
Cora is furious
when I tell her
where I went

Takemura-san's? the man with the stick?
why didn't you take me?
I solved the crime as much as you!
I was the one actually listening to him!

after my bath
Cora tries to keep me out of ~~my~~ our room
hiding my box of international coins
which I search for and know is missing
the second I finally barge in

so I scoop up
stuffed animals as hostages
and go outside to the laundry balcony
and threaten to drop them over the edge
to the dark ground below

she screams
Dad comes up
yells at me
and sends me
downstairs to wash
      all the dinner dishes
      the rice cooker
      and even the smelly
      composter pot

when I go up later
Cora is the one who says sorry
so after a while
I sit down in the cave
of her lower bunk
and tell her about
Takemura-san

how sometimes his speech is clear
but other times not
how his mouth scowls
from the Parkinson's
how he gets stuck
and can't move
and how his daughter
was there and showed me
how to put my foot
crosswise in front of his

to make his leg think
it has to step up and over I tell Cora
which gets him moving

in our bedroom
I show her the way
that Takemura-san's feet
seemed glued to the floor

then I make her
put her foot
crosswise to one of mine
and I unstick my foot
and step over

I don't tell Cora
how weird it felt
being there in a stranger's house
in the home of a scowling old man
or how at his kitchen table
I wanted to escape
as I listened so hard
but couldn't understand
even after he repeated words
again and again

until finally his loud daughter came in
      the one who'd been standing with
      hands on hips after the fire
and served us barley tea
and explained things
like the crosswise foot
and that her father doesn't smile
because of the disease
and that he looks angry but isn't
and that it's okay to ask him
to repeat his words
again and again
and again

it's like a miracle Cora whispers
your foot making the top of a T
across his foot
the way it makes
his stuck foot think
it can move

I don't know about a miracle
maybe more like a brain leap
like mind over matter

but then I'm thinking

   what if someone's not with him?
   how long does he stay stuck
   before his feet
   move forward again?

Chapter 15

RESOURCES

weekends are so much better than weeks
because they start with double aikido
on Saturday morning
then soccer in the park
and Sunday is a family hike
then chores and homework

but weekdays
follow weekends
and Sunday nights
I have to center myself
and prepare to return
to the Dragon's Mouth

it's not actually called
Dragon's Mouth anymore
that name goes way back
to when the school was connected
to Dragon's Mouth temple

now the school's called
Ridge Way Elementary or
Ridgeline Pass Elementary
or however you want to
translate the Japanese

but Dragon's Mouth
seems a better fit
to me

this Monday at school
I manage to hold my center
all day long

but by the time Mom and Cora pick me up
I feel like I've been at the dojo for six hours

      alert
      ready every second
      my whole body trembling
      from concentration
      and exertion

I sleep all the way to Yokohama

in English group
the olders and youngers both
are still doing economics
supply and demand
goods and services

then we olders have to look at photos
and decide which are the

> human
> natural
> or capital
> resources

and teach the youngers

I'm so tired of this unit
and can't wait to start the next
on marine ecosystems
and intertidal life
since Mom promises to take us
down the coast of Miura
to a place where the tide pools
are full of everything—

> anemones
> crabs
> sea slugs that squirt purple
> urchins and abalone
> and sometimes
> an octopus

but Trina's mom announces
that we're extending this unit
another couple weeks
for a special project

Trina and Ami seem happy
since they think they want to start
their own business
in fashion or shoes

but Nenita, Will, and I groan
and use our capital resource—our brains—
to petition the parents to also extend
the marine unit by two weeks

and we win

hah!

Chapter 16

BROOMS

just like Monday
Tuesday morning
at school goes okay
so long as I'm always
      on alert

but when lunch recess ends
I discover

      someone has taken
      my indoor shoes

it's not the first time
and I know the places
I can look:
> toilets
> tops of high cabinets
> first graders' cubbies

but it's cleaning time
and I'm late
so I head
to the music room
in my socks

and late means
the brooms and mop
are already taken
and I'm stuck again
with the dustpan

in the music room
desks have been pushed aside
Naho and Yuki are sweeping
Mika's riding a mop
and Shunta and Gō
have unscrewed and removed
both of the wide broom heads
and they're running around
waving the long handles
like samurai swords

cleaning in socks? Shunta says
        in fake surprise
no indoor shoes? Gō says
        slicing the air above my head

Shunta points to a dust pile
and commands me to
sweep it
into my dustpan

to use a dustpan
you have to squat down
and as soon
as you start to sweep
into the pan
you lose your center
and you can be whacked
on the butt
with a broom
or mopped
on the head

the question is
      whether to duck
      and roll out of the way
      or not

Naho taunts
missed a spot she says

I sweep

here
she points
and here
faster and faster

I sweep up dust pile
after dust pile
then Yuki
starts pointing at random

do it
she says

I don't

and suddenly
a broom handle
cracks on my head
just above my ear

I drop the brush and dustpan
put one hand to my head
and keep my other hand
      fisted
      ready

for the rest of cleaning
I just sit on a desk
in the corner
my back to the wall
facing them all

it's not bleeding much
but I smear it over my palm
so they can see

and finally
they leave me alone

Mom yells at me
for my filthy socks
and makes me scrub them
and hang them out myself

I don't tell her
about my missing indoor shoes
finally found with the guest slippers
at the front school entrance

I don't tell her about the lump
on the side of my head that I dab
with a soapy washcloth before rinsing
and climbing into the tub

I don't tell her that the floor
in our school is filthy
because brooms are not so much used
for sweeping

I don't tell her
because I don't want her
interfering at school
making things in the Dragon's Mouth
        even worse

Chapter 17

DANGO

on Wednesday
at the after-school center
I take off my shoes
nod to the women
in the closet office
and search for Cora

in one room, two boys are
climbing over stacks of foam blocks
in another room, four kids
play soccer with a book
in a third room, kids hurl a rubber ball
high speed, wall to wall

I slide open the doors
to the backyard
step down and into
some plastic sandals

across the yard
I can see Cora
in the sandpit
making *dango*

not *dango* to eat—
      gluey balls of *mochi*
       with sweet sauces on top—
but *doro dango*
mud *dango*

      dirt balls

Cora is a *doro dango* expert
ever since preschool

in the back garden at home
there are always *dango*
decorated with flower petals
or blades of grass or leaves
or sprinkled with dry sand
or topped with a red berry

Cora's *Doro Dango* Recipe
fill a cup of water
from a tap
dampen dark sand
scoop a handful
to mold
add more sand
smooth it
add more sand
smooth it
and smooth it
to form a perfect sphere

each takes five minutes or more
and sometimes they break

another girl is with her
in the yard making *dango*
and they have ten *dango*
lined up along a tree root

wow, you made lots
I say to her in Japanese
knowing better than to speak to her
in English in front of a friend

un—yeah, she says

let's go I say in Japanese

mada—not yet, she says

she's polishing a *dango*

I wait awhile longer
say *let's go* again
and once more she says *mada!*
so I switch to English

we won't have time for an adventure

she smooths the *dango*
gently sets it down
by the tree root
where it promptly splits

I think we're stuck here
for another ten minutes
but the other girl
hands her a leaf

Cora thanks her
sets the leaf
over the crack
and turns to me to go

she doesn't speak to me in English
until we're outside
practically halfway up the hill
to our neighborhood

it's better there in the garden she says

then she shifts back into
her pain-in-the-neck sister self

what's our adventure today
it better not be just a park
and it better not be a fire
do you even have a plan today?

when I don't answer
she says *see?*

so I start walking fast uphill
which is pretty impossible since
the road is so steep there are
circles cut in the concrete
to keep cars from slipping

we trudge ahead
crest the hill
run down the other side
turn left at our road
climb again to our house

and inside on the table
in the kitchen
is a note
two cups
two bananas
and some coins

> Drink some water
> eat the bananas
> then you can buy snacks
> at the futon shop.
> But save enough money to buy
> milk on your way home!
> xoxoxoxoxoxo
> Mom

Cora cheers
and we eat our bananas
fast

the futon shop
where we park our bikes
is Cora's favorite shop
because this futon shop
doesn't sell only
futons, pillows, and blankets
but also *dagashi* candies

      soda-flavored sours
      chocolate soccer balls
      whistle candy gum
      mini ramens
      candy colas
      teeny *mochi* squares
      gummi-rope
      even mini *dango*

Cora thinks and thinks
and picks up and puts down
every single type of candy

hurry up I say
or the adventure's off

at last
she puts
her candies
with mine
in the mini basket
and we pay
the futon lady

then we stuff the candies
into our pockets
get on our bikes
and I lead the way to the port

thinking we can eat our candies
on the breakwater
watching the sea
as the sun drops

good plan, right?

Chapter 18

BREAKWATER

we ride past storage buildings
heaps of fish nets
and boats pulled up
onto wooden boards
on the concrete ramp
all the way out to the breakwater
where we park our bikes

Cora's wary
we're not supposed to be here
Dad said no water she says

we won't be in the water I say
just near it

to get up onto the high part
of the breakwater
you have to charge at the wall
and keep running up

I show Cora
and make it up
on my second try

Cora runs hard
but slips
back
         down

after three tries
I lie down on the
breakwater
and reach low
to pull her up

we walk along the top
of the sea wall above
the open water with waves
sloshing gently below us

the sky is pinkish gray
the sea fairly still
and all along the wall
people are fishing

we walk around and over
tackle boxes and coolers
rods and lines until
one fisherman grunts at us

then with cold eyes he says
you shouldn't be here
and way too late I notice
standing beside him

Yuki

at first I think of the cousin
who set the fire
and wonder if it's him
but then I remember *he*

was sent to jail
so this man must be
her father or brother
or another cousin

Yuki makes a face
at us, as cold
as the guy's eyes
and says

        nothing

the man points
with his chin
at a ladder
that goes down
to the lower level . . . huh?

we have the right to be up there
as much as they do, or rather
they're not supposed to be there
as much as we're not supposed to

but his eyes are like ice
so I lead Cora down the ladder
and direct her to the lighthouse
at the end of the lower wall

I don't even pause at the lighthouse
just turn right around to go back
but we just got here! Cora says
you can't rush an adventure!

I don't care
I don't want to be anywhere
near Yuki or her brother
or whoever he is

though I know Cora knows
I'm just making it up I say
we have one more thing to do
but we won't have time if we stay here

Cora doesn't argue
just follows me to our bikes
and we ride away from the port
and all the people fishing

> I hate
> that I can't seem to get
> away from school
> even after school

> I hate
> that seeing Yuki
> has ruined my day

I stop at a park
and do some pull-ups
and push-ups
to let off some steam

Cora does the trick
flipping over the metal bar
that little kids learn
in Japanese school
that I can't do
and we ride the swings
and leap off
again and again
until I don't care
about Yuki

then Cora squints, says
was this the one more thing?

while I'm thinking she says
there isn't a one more thing, is there?

there is I say

we get back on our bikes
and as we ride I think
and think some more
up along the river
past the three bridges
then it hits me—
I take her to the section
with the earthen path
and we lock our bikes
beside the wall

      what are we doing? she asks
visiting I say

      who? she says
Takemura-san I say and ring the bell

      Cora grabs my arm
      do Mom and Dad know we're here?
      did you bring a gift?
      you're supposed to have a gift
      if you visit someone!
shh! I say

when the door opens
he stands before us
scowling in the door frame
and Cora shrinks back

ah! he says, recognizing us

excuse me I say
I know when you said the other day
to visit again you didn't mean
today, but . . .

Come in! he says . . . *shōgi board . . .*
in here . . . your first lesson? . . . sister, too?
I try to catch his words
tell him yes to *shōgi*
but a *very* quick lesson
since we have to be home
by five o'clock on the dot

right, well, young lady with me . . .
boy . . . against us

in the living room
I kneel down by the wooden board
while Takemura-san motions
for Cora to sit by him

he starts to hand her *koma* pieces
larger pieces . . . more power he says
in that slurring mumbly voice
this is ōshō *. . . in English . . .* king?

Cora, still standing beside him
reaches into her jeans pocket
and sets out three wrapped
whistle gum circles

these are for you she says
ah, thank you he says
and bows solemnly
later . . . shall we?

Cora nods and finally
sits down beside him
as he sets the gum candies
on a side table

Takemura-san points
to *kanji* characters
on each *koma* piece
kanji that I mostly know

the king goes here, middle . . . this row

I copy their setup
on my side of the *shōgi* grid
and when the board is ready
he explains the moves

except I can't understand
quite what he's saying
though it seems to be something
about building a castle

I figure we can look it up later
for now I'm just glad to listen
and try to understand
this *shōgi* world
  ōshō, *hisha*, and *ryūma*—
   king, flying chariot, dragon horse

I don't look at Cora
I know I've tricked her
this isn't what she had in mind
for an adventure

but when I finally
glance at her after I
try a move to outwit them
she looks up at me

smiling

now this is an adventure!
she whispers in English

and I smile back
relieved to be away
from Yuki, Shunta, and Gō
trying to build my castle

Chapter 19

EFFORT

it's calmer in *han* six now
and I think it's probably because
I didn't rat on anyone about my
broom-smacked head

I hold my center in class
stay focused at my desk
      on my work sheets
      and on the members
      of *han* six

always ready
to divert a punch
or duck a hit

Ōshima-sensei
is going on and on these days
about why he thinks judo
like kendo
is a good thing

because nowadays
they are holding judo classes
in middle schools
including our own
local middle school

I don't say it out loud
but I want to know

     why not aikido?

in aikido we're getting ready
to perform the moves we'll do
next month in a full-day
demonstration

there aren't really meets
or competitions in aikido
just a show of how far
we've advanced in a year

hundreds of kids
of all sizes in white *gi*
and all colored belts
holding their centers

so . . .
why not aikido?

they say you can't start a fight
with aikido
only finish one

you can't really attack
or punch
or kick

you just push
or pull
or twist

to turn the energy
and throw the other person
       off center

at the dojo
some kids think
that the chanting
and the breathing
and the silence
at the beginning
is dull and boring

but that's when I know
I've shed my problems
left them all
with my pile of clothes
in the changing room

when I tie the belt
when I kneel at the threshold
when I bow to the sensei
before the framed calligraphy for
ki—氣—life force, energy
when I'm prepared to practice the moves
all of Dragon's Mouth
disappears

on weekends I can easily
get up early for aikido
get up early for family hikes
or a museum or watching Cora
but during the week
I hate getting out of bed

Mom says I'm uneven lately
asks me what's going on
tries to talk to me
tells me to make a list
of the parts of my week
from best to worst

like days of the week? I ask

*like activities, school
tutoring, English group
everything* she says

so here's my week
in a list
best to worst

aikido
weekend hikes and stuff
English group
Friday soccer
babysitting Cora
tutor time
dinner
breakfast
homework
school

then she says
now do the same with school
break it down
best to worst

so I do
and write

      science
      everything else

she says
explain

I shrug

what can I say?
it's not like I have a choice
to go or not go
to that school

there's nothing to explain I say

she sighs and gives up
on trying to get me to talk
and says *I think you need to make
more effort, Jason Parker*

on Monday after school
when Mom and Cora
pick me up for English group
Mom eyes me
before she puts the car
in drive

but nothing major happened
just a couple of head whacks
and one slam into a wall

so I look out the window
and soon fall asleep

at English group
I can forget it all

even if we're learning
about entrepreneurs
their failures
their successes

at least we get to eat
chocolate bars
as we study
Milton Hershey

and chew on
milk caramels
as we study
Taichiro Morinaga

thinking about
benefits, costs
risks, and rewards

the English group homework
is to think like an entrepreneur
and come up with a good or service
and a complete business plan

Cora and Mom
talk all the way home
and all through dinner

Mom keeps saying
what about you, J?
what are your ideas?

but honestly
I'm thinking more like
an inventor
than an entrepreneur

thinking I need to create
an invisible helmet for my head
and special glasses
for seeing 360 degrees

my idea
I finally say

is a program for
aikido in every neighborhood
aikido in every school

Mom gives me a long look

I'm listening, J
whenever you want to talk

about what?
I quickly say

because I can't imagine
life would get better
if Mom talked to
Ōshima-sensei
and stirred things up
in the Dragon's Mouth

things are fine I say
I just need to make
more effort

Chapter 20

WAVES

sixth graders are in charge
of the bowling stall
at the Games and Play Day
coming up in mid-November

we've collected plastic bottles
decorated them with colored tape
so little kids can knock them
over with tennis balls, and now

we spend a whole class
arguing over the rules
while Ōshima-sensei
grades our homework

without thinking, I speak up
I suggest we create prizes
because that's how it worked
at my school in the U.S. once
when the PTA held a fair

but Shunta whacks me
and Mika laughs too loud
saying *we don't need prizes*
everyone just plays to play
so I keep quiet the rest of the day

we have two weeks to plan what to put
on the signs, how to arrange plastic bottles
and distances for lines for different age kids
all of which could be done in an hour
if everyone just stopped arguing

I've decided
I won't contribute
won't say a word
they can do without my help

at recess I don't go outside
I just read manga in the library

this week it's raining
when I pick up Cora
from the after-school center
and find her in the main room
throwing cushion blocks
at three other kids

she's out of breath
from chasing kids
to whack them
and from escaping
being whacked

outside trudging up the hill
wrestling with our umbrellas
in wind that's blowing rain
exactly sideways she says
she *had* to play that way
she'd tried drawing
but kids kept hitting her

I'm tired and thirsty she says
what's our adventure?

this time I really don't know
since it's raining
and I didn't plan on rain
only good weather
in which case I'd planned to
      cross the bridge to the island
      walk up to the shrine
      maybe as far as the
      supposed dragon cave

as we eat bananas and rice crackers
we watch TV weather
      satellite images
      precipitation projections
      and warnings
      about waves

when I see six meters for our coast
I watch the whole report again
paying close attention
because now I see a typhoon
in the corner of the screen
moving toward us
pushing rain, and wind, and waves—
      and I know what our adventure will be

rain suits
I say to Cora
and she looks at me funny

I say *six-meter waves*
we've got to see them

we're not supposed to go to the beach
even in good weather! she says

I pull on my rain pants and jacket
that Mom bought for our hikes

we won't go onto the beach I say
just a high place for watching waves

boots she suggests
but neither of us has boots that fit
so we pull on the rain suits
and our already wet sneakers

we unlock our bikes
and coast downhill
with typhoon rain
pelting our faces

along the streetcar line
we are practically
the only ones
out on bicycles

and we are definitely
the only ones
out on the road
by the beach

where the wind

    slams us
full force
  wobbling
 our bikes

we pedal down
the coast road sidewalk
but I hadn't counted on
rain lashing us
so hard it hurts

at the crossing light
we fight against gusts
walking our bikes across the road
to the landing of concrete stairs
that lead down to the beach

and there, high above sand
and waves that we can barely see
we hold our handlebars
in the punching
howling wind

below us, surf
pounds the beach
so hard it's like being
inside thunder

salt spray
tropical wind
and rain
slap us

and just
standing there
        or trying to
we're nearly
drowning

Cora shouts, but I can't hear
so we turn our bikes around
on that beach stair landing
        and there

by the crossing light
in an oversized
clear plastic raincoat
        is a kid

he's wearing flip flops
and his raincoat
flaps and snaps wildly
        and under the raincoat

he's wearing shorts
a sweatshirt
and I think
        binoculars

164

he presses the crossing button
and when the light changes
the wind
thrusts us all

        fast across the road

we don't ride
just push our bikes
to escape that beach
the gusting salt
rain and sand

and when we turn inland
to the main street
between buildings
I shout to Cora
you okay?

she nods
but she's frowning
and her eyes say
this is so NOT
a good adventure

the boy steps around us
shouts above the wind *this way!*
and beyond a noodle shop
he leads us off the road
to a streetcar crossing
that doesn't have a gate

we're so wet and nearly drowned
that we follow, watching
and listening for trains
as I carry my bike
and the kid carries Cora's bike
over the streetcar rails

he motions for us to
lean them against a wall
then beckons for us to follow
through a tile-roofed gate
and suddenly we are in a garden
and the big gate door

is latching behind us

Chapter 21

HOT TEA

before us is an old house
palms bending in the wind
and a tall stone lantern
beside a pebble path

the kid leads us up the path
past a huge pottery urn
catching plopping rain
and into a stone-floored entryway

we are so soaking wet
even inside our rain suits
that not even Cora
hesitates to step inside

the kid leaves us there
dripping puddles
onto the floor

returns with towels
and tells us to take off our shoes
and rain suits

so we towel off
then he motions for us
to step up into the house

which we almost do
but I stop
because I realize

now that he's out of his raincoat
the kid is actually older than me
maybe much older

and I don't think
anyone else is here
in this quiet house

but Cora steps up
follows him into the kitchen
where he turns on a burner
starts heating water
and spoons tea
into a teapot

do you go to the middle school?
I ask from the doorway

he tilts his head
points to a chair
for me to sit in
says *no*, nothing more

high school? I ask

no

well what school DO you go to?
Cora asks

I don't he says
but if I did I'd be
third year middle school

the kid mutters about
searching for rice crackers

why don't you go to school? Cora asks

he shrugs and says
I study at home . . .
do you like hōjicha?

any tea's fine I say

so, do you? Cora asks the kid

what? make hōjicha? he says

no, study! do you study at home?

he thinks a minute then says
mostly no

and we all laugh

he moves aside his wet binoculars
and pours the tea into cups
as Cora and I sit down at the table

I'm Cora Cora says
pronouncing it the Japanese way
so it sounds like "cola"
and this is my brother Jason
but most people call him J

the kid nods, that's all
till Cora sticks her head out
like a bird, expectant
and finally he gets the hint
and says

I'm Daiki
Nakano Daiki

like he's out of practice
saying his own name

we sit without talking awhile
just sipping hot tea, then he says
I watched you going to the beach
I wanted to make sure you didn't
go down the stairs to the water
people do that sometimes
check out the waves and try surfing
even in weather like this
people drown, you know

I say
we were just looking

he nods
not believing
like he knows everything
like I could have been one of those people
going too close to the waves

and Cora is looking at him
like he's her big hero

really I say
we were just looking

but Daiki continues

last year after I quit school
I started watching the water
when the weather's rough

one time
like today
before a typhoon
I watched a surfer go out
but he got tossed all over
and disappeared
so I called emergency

by the time firefighters
arrived with rescue stuff
he'd been under too long
and they couldn't revive him

he died? Cora says, and Daiki nods

didn't you call 119? Cora asks

of course he says

and they couldn't help him? Cora whispers

and this Daiki guy says coldly
no, they can't do everything, you know

and I'm thinking it's time to leave
but Cora goes cold right back at him
changes the topic, and says
I think you should return to school

Daiki snorts
not that school
and he jerks his head
and by the direction and his eyes
I know he's talking about
the local middle school
the one I'll go to
if we can't afford
international school

why? I say

see this? he says
and shows me a scar
on his forehead
near his hairline
that's from when they tried
to shove me into the toilet
head first

so what happened? I ask

what do you mean? he says

were those kids punished?

they made them apologize Daiki says
made them clean bathrooms

so then it got better? I say

no he says
it got worse

after tea
before Cora and I leave

Daiki and I
trade cell phone numbers

so, maybe see you again?
Daiki says

and Cora and I both say
yeah, see you again

Chapter 22

TYPHOON DAY

the next day there is no school
because the typhoon moves toward us
faster than expected, and there are

    flood warnings

    landslide warnings

    and the wind is blowing

        garden furniture

                branches

        shutters

                    signs

and I guess the principal
figures it's a good idea
not to have any accidents

    at least not from natural causes

Mom's and Dad's
classes are canceled
aikido's canceled
so we are all home
with rain shutters closed
and even though it's
midday in October
it's like a hot summer night
inside our house

the bell cricket
drives us crazy
singing *rin rin rin*
from the kitchen table
where we set the cage to keep it
from drowning on the balcony

and throughout the day
we find inside the house
escaping the rain
 one lizard
 one huge spider
 one gecko
 and two big cockroaches
 that I chase and—*thwap!*

Mom puts on a Tora-san DVD
from a collection Dad got for her birthday
and first it's just her watching
         then Cora and her
         then Cora, me, and her
         then Cora, me, Dad, and her

all the Tora-san films are similar—
this weird guy Tora-san
sells trinkets and stuff
in different parts of Japan
and wants a girlfriend
but doesn't get one

Mom says Tora-san
is good for her Japanese
and even though the films
are kind of old and dumb
whenever she puts one on
I can't help but watch

in this episode
Tora-san takes his first flight
all the way to Okinawa
to see his girlfriend who's sick

he helps her get well
but doesn't stay

and at the end of the movie
all of us decide we, too
want to take a flight
to the southern islands

and Cora asks
if that's possible
or if we could take a train
all the way to Kyūshū
then take a ferry
to that tropical island
where they sing
and eat outside
and where the beach sand
is perfect and clean

Mom's happy face turns serious again
maybe—IF I get a full-time position she says

and Dad says
well, probably not a train
but maybe we could drive
then he pulls out his phone
and looks up drive time
from Tōkyō to Kagoshima
and says it would take us
eighteen hours each way
and the gas and tolls
would cost a fortune
and I know right away
this trip won't happen
not with their schedules
and the cost of our visits
to the States each summer

and everyone knows
we can't afford the trip anyway
but no one says why—that
we're saving money for me
to change schools

we still don't have the money
for international school, do we I say

and Mom says to be patient
that we'll have it soon
that since she's teaching
the Wednesday classes
on top of her other classes
all different days of the week
we'll have the tuition
for the fall

fall? I say
but elementary school graduation
is in March!

they look at each other and Dad says
that actually, because Japanese school
ends in March and starts in April
yet the international school year
ends in June and starts in late August
that means from April until the start
of the international school year
I might be homeschooled or something

or something? I say
you mean, like
go to the local middle school?
no way!
why can't I just start
international school in April?

Jason Mom says all soft and quiet
like I'm being unreasonable
besides tuition you have to pay
a big registration fee
and given the cost
we think that rather than start
at the end of their school year
it makes more sense to start
at the start of their school year
with all the other new students

and suddenly I think of Daiki—
how he doesn't go to school
and I ask
how old do you have to be to quit school?

my parents look at me funny

then Cora opens her big mouth and says
yeah! that boy we met yesterday
at the beach
he doesn't go to school
that's illegal isn't it!

the beach?
Mom and Dad both say

and Cora clamps
both her hands
over her mouth

     too late

Chapter 23

WHITE DEER

that night we're
lying in our beds
and I'm not talking to Cora
but she's yakking and yakking
at me

I already had to listen to
a lecture about water
a lecture about my responsibilities
a lecture about strangers
a lecture about thinking about Cora

and I'm tired of thinking about Cora
so I don't answer

she's jabbering on and on
and I'm not listening and
shove my head under my pillow
but she climbs the ladder to my bunk

she lifts the pillow
money! she says
I'm talking about money
so listen

she tells me her business plan
for us to take pictures
of the beach and Mount Fuji
of temples and shrines
with her stuffed squirrel
named Gray in each photo

get it? she says
it's like Gray
is a tourist
visiting Japan
taking a trip around Kamakura
and this whole area

I lift the pillow
all the way off my head
and stare at her
and what exactly will we
do with these pictures of Gray?

sell them!
make postcards!
make folders!

I groan
how? and why?
and WHO would want pictures
of a stuffed squirrel? I say

I don't know!
YOU think of that—
I thought up the product
YOU do the marketing

right I tell her
and finally
she climbs down the ladder
and leaves me alone

the typhoon wakes us both
in the middle of the night
with wind that screams and
gusts that hit with such force
they make the house shudder

in between gusts
there's a steady roar
which I finally realize
                is the ocean
way down the hill
as loud as if it's
outside our door

Cora comes up to my bunk
and in the typhoon night
things rattle, crash
smash, slam
and groan

finally we take our pillows
into Mom and Dad's room
and wriggle into their futons
then we all give up sleeping
go down to the living room
and watch TV news of the storm

until the power cuts off

then we're in the dark
pointing our flashlights
setting up the camping lantern
opening the sofa bed
that we bought when we moved here
for visitors from the States
who never seem to visit
and we squish in together
and in the lantern light
we listen to Dad tell a story

a story he learned
in Massachusetts
when he was a boy

Dad's story
      which he says may
      or may not be true
      is about a white deer
      considered sacred to Mohicans
      a deer that came in the early morning
      and at dusk to drink from a lake

      and a French fur trader
      who wanted very badly
      the skin of that white deer
      but the tribal leaders wouldn't
      give it up and guarded the deer
      and its fawn which was
      also white

      until one night
      one member of the tribe betrayed them
      took the white deer to the Frenchman
      who killed it and skinned it
      and set off for Canada
      which was the way to get to France
      in those days

Cora whimpers *he killed it? he killed the white deer?*

yes, sweetie, I'm sorry Dad says

what about the fawn?

just listen Dad says

> after the white deer
> was killed and taken away
> all good fortune ended
> there was famine
> and illness in the valley
> there were battles
> and crop blights
>
> but they say that the fawn
> just may have survived
> and that years later a hunter
> near the lake saw a white deer
> and took aim with his gun
> but the birds cried out
> and squirrels chattered
> and his dog barked
> alerting the deer to run

and they say that even today
if you go hiking there
in the valley near the lake
you might catch sight
of not a white-tailed deer
but an all-white deer

and they say that, to this day
all the animals in that valley
will do anything
to protect their deer
and that hunters
near that lake
never succeed
in bagging deer

that's a sad story Cora says
and Mom rubs her back

then Dad goes on
telling us the story
of some white deer
that came to listen
when Mugaku Sogen
a Buddhist priest from China
gave his first sermon
in the late 1200s
at the temple Engakuji
right here in Kamakura . . .

and the four of us, lined up
not very comfortably
on the too-narrow sofa bed
all thinking of white deer
start to doze

waking up whenever
          something cracks
          or the house shakes
          or branches rake across
          the rain shutters

Chapter 24

HAMMER

when the phone rings too early
to tell us school will be delayed
the wind is still roaring
but morning light squeezes in
between rain shutter gaps

Dad opens a window
slides back a shutter
so we can see the road
full of
      branches, garden pots
       roofing and debris
and into the house
blows hot salty air

the power comes on again
the TV startles us
and the satellite image shows
the knot of typhoon
just northeast of us

so we all go back to sleep
but in our own
beds and futons

because of the delay
the school day is short
and afterward
Yōhei, Shō, and I
walk down to the beach
to survey the damage

the typhoon has wrecked the coast—
fishing sheds
and seaweed shacks
are in ruins
and people are busy
making piles of debris

I ask a woman if she needs help
and she hands me some cotton gloves
gestures at all the mess
and at the destroyed sheds

sort it into piles
she says
pointing to mounds of
      usable stuff
      bits of wood
      plastics
      cans
      other garbage

so we go at the mess
of logs and plastic junk
shoes, seaweed, plants
dead fish, pottery, and bottles

it's salty humid
the air is clearing
the sun's beating down
and everything's starting to stink

and way off in the distance
apart from everyone
picking through debris
I see Daiki

I work my way down the beach
away from Yōhei and Shō
making it seem like I hadn't
known Daiki was there

hi I say *thanks for the tea the other day*
I was going to call you . . .
he nods, tosses a bloated fish
what a mess I add, and he nods again

I go back to picking up junk
throwing it on piles
but Daiki's looking at me—
you speak English, right? he says

yeah I say, and he's about to say more
but then his face clouds
seeing someone approaching
from somewhere behind me

Wednesday, my house
okay? he mutters
then ducks and moves away
as Yōhei approaches

were you talking to him? Yōhei says

yeah I say

well, don't, he's a jerk

I stare at Yōhei
what do you mean?

he's just weird
he was in my brother's grade
but he doesn't go to school now
people think he's crazy

well, people talk that way about me I say

no, they don't
they just make fun of you
because you're different
that's all

I drop my armload
of typhoon trash
right at Yōhei's feet
and walk away

from him
  from the beach
    across the coast road
      up to the streetcar tracks
        and into the lanes
          that lead up our hill

I'm halfway home
when I realize
I'm still wearing
the fisherwoman's cotton gloves

I throw them in some bushes

after aikido on Saturday
I stay in—
I don't go out for soccer
I don't ride around on my bike

I just hang out at home
help Dad clean up the
typhoon-messed garden
and do English homework

I message Daiki
to tell him
I'll definitely be there
on Wednesday

just different, that's all
Yōhei said

      like that makes it okay
      to hammer me down

Chapter 25

SHŌNAN GRAY

Sunday is a Gray day
taking pictures with Cora
all over Kamakura
posing that stupid
stuffed squirrel
everywhere—

    riding the streetcar
    in front of the Great Buddha
    at a shop with a cone of
    green and purple ice cream

in English group on Monday
the parents are all excited
about the pictures I took
and about Cora's business plan
which I'm suddenly
somehow a big
important part of

other kids have simpler business ideas

dog walking services
calendars with recipes
English lessons
muffin sales

Cora's idea
is Shōnan Gray, and the plan
is to take photographs
of Gray and our Shōnan Coast
then add English
and put pictures and text
on T-shirts
dog-poop bags
mugs
clear folders

>*Shōnan Gray sees the Great Buddha*
>*Shōnan Gray eats an ice cream*
>*Shōnan Gray wants to surf*
>*Shōnan Gray rides the streetcar*

to me it's stupid
but she's the CEO
and I'm the CFO
and chief of photography

at least I like the spreadsheet job
setting up the functions
so we can track income
and expenses

at school I make extra effort
to keep my mouth shut
trying not to be different
trying not to be hammered

but then on Tuesday
something goes missing
and at first, because of the way
Ōshima-sensei's talking

I can't figure out
what it is exactly
and I open my big mouth
　　　　to ask

Ōshima-sensei holds up
a plain bronze paperweight—*bunchin*—
and I realize that what's missing
is the dragon paperweight

but the way Ōshima-sensei
said *bunchin* is hilarious to Naho
who imitates with

    a pen

    an eraser

    a protractor

then gets the brilliant idea
to draw a heap of *unchi*—poop
and hold up the drawing in one hand
her calligraphy paperweight in the other
and looks from one to the other
and in an Ōshima-sensei voice says

    bunchin

    unchi

I laugh
because I have to
but I hate
that I have to laugh

and then
Ōshima-sensei
hollers at *han* six
and we all
have to write
bunchin—paperweight—文鎮
in our notebooks
fifty times
and *ryū*—dragon
old style 龍
and *ryū*—dragon
new style 竜
fifty times each

which I don't mind
because for a change
everyone in *han* six is
actually working

Chapter 26

BOSSES

on Wednesday Cora has made
Shōnan Gray plans
    to ring the big bronze bell
    at the Dragon's Mouth Temple
    for *Shōnan Gray rings the bell*

but I tell her that our plans
have been revised:
    we're going to Daiki's
    so we'll take pictures
    somewhere near his house

Cora has a fit about this
and says she's the CEO and
screams *you're not the boss of me!*
as we get on our bikes

when we stop for a car to pass
I tell her that maybe I'm not the boss of her
but as director of photography
I control the photo shoots

and she huffs
and rides off
pedaling like a lunatic
ahead of me

I shout at her to stop
and try to overtake her
but then I slow down and just follow
when I realize she's actually

riding the route to Daiki's

Daiki is waiting by the tracks
and he carries Cora's bike across
leads us into the garden
and closes the gate

why's it always so quiet here?
do you live alone? Cora asks
looking around the yard and entry
don't you have a family?

Cora! I warn, but Daiki answers
my grandfather and father are working
my sister's married, my mother's dead
and my brother's sick—
        he's at a hospital

Cora stands still, mouth gaping

sick? I ask
like cancer or something?
and now Cora warns—*Jason!*

but Daiki says
no, mentally sick
and I think of what Yōhei said

in the kitchen Daiki makes us tea
and gives us each
a big hard rice cracker
the thick noisy kind that
take time to crunch on

finally when we are all
cracker quiet he says *so . . .*
why I called you here—
I need to learn English
since my grandfather
wants to send me to Hawaii
to go to a school there
and stay with some relative

Hawaii! Cora says

I'm studying online he says
but I have to reach the test level
for that school, so I need a tutor
but now there's no money
so anyway, do you have time?

I'm surprised
thinking this over
and Cora's kicking me
under the table
glaring at me
meaning *say yes!*

but I'm thinking of the business model
and how you shouldn't give away
services for free so I say
maybe we could trade
maybe you could help us
with our business

so Cora explains Shōnan Gray
and I say that I think it's dumb
but we need to think of places to take Gray
> scenic places
> historic sites
and local specialties for Gray to try

Daiki thinks that dumb or not
Gray stuff really could sell
and he reminds us that behind his house
is the famous ancient temple
where, in 1185, warrior Minamoto no Yoshitsune
wrote his really famous letter
to his brother the ruler, Minamoto no Yoritomo
begging him to allow him back into
Kamakura City, or so the legend goes

hey! we could put a pencil
in the squirrel's paw I say
and pose it with some paper for
> *Shōnan Gray writes a letter*

> and I can't believe
> I'm saying this

Daiki gets a pencil and paper
and we head for that temple
famous for that letter
that didn't work because the ruler Yoritomo
never did let his brother back into the capital
but instead sent him away
turned against him, and sent retainers
to bring back his head

and Daiki is telling us this story
and how the head was identified
right in this neighborhood
and Cora is all grossed out
especially when Daiki's saying
the head was so decomposed
that in fact they still don't know for sure
if it was Yoshitsune's or not and who knows
maybe he escaped to Mongolia
and became Genghis Khan

but as we're talking and walking
along the short bit of road
between the turn in the streetcar tracks
and the entrance to the temple
we run into Shunta and Gō

Shunta's on his racing bike
which is really amazing
with all the painted lightning bolts
and thin stripes and details
some of which I think are new—
       tongues of flame
         running up and wrapping around
       the forks

Gō is on a rusted mountain bike
and I'm thinking how maybe I could
turn the energy, avert a scene here
by complimenting Shunta
suggesting he paint Gō's bike

but they're laughing
exaggerated and loud
just from seeing Daiki
      with us

there are comments
I don't quite get
but get well enough
      about crazies and hospitals

Daiki's hands
turn to fists

we keep walking
and I decide this isn't the time
to talk of painting bikes

because when we turn
uphill to the temple approach
Shunta and Gō still follow

we wander near the bronze bell
the one we ring at New Year's
and we linger by the cave mouth
then stand near the main hall
but Shunta and Gō shadow us
whichever way we turn

Cora keeps Gray in her backpack
I keep Mom's camera in my pocket
Daiki hides the pencil and paper
and none of us says a word

they follow us even when we leave the temple
without having taken a single picture of Gray

by Daiki's house Cora and I get our bikes
and with no more words between us
  not even confirming the day
  for studying English
Daiki goes into his garden
and locks the gate behind him

Cora and I ride off
and when we lose Shunta and Gō
we ride to the futon shop
pool our allowance
and buy a heap
of *dagashi* candies
that we eat at home—
  tiny squares of colored *mochi*
  morocco yogurt
  coated chocolates in a circle
  and mini colas

I try to distract Cora between bites
make her say her times table
in English and Japanese
but she keeps saying *I hate those boys!*
I hate them—why do they get to be
the bosses of everyone?

Chapter 27

EVIDENCE

in school there are long lectures
about stealing and honesty
and pleas for whoever
took the dragon paperweight
>   that has been at the school
>   used in that classroom for twenty years
>   and which forms a pair with the dragon
>   in the other sixth-grade classroom
>   which is not missing
to speak up and come clean

but no one does

some say the dragons keep away
the ghosts of soldiers who died
in the school when it was used
as a hospital during the war

the ghosts that the principal
always tells us we might meet
if we stay too late at school
after everyone's gone home

and I'm not saying I believe him
but when everyone's gone home
and you have to return to school
because you forgot something

it's creepy, quiet, and still
so we all want
that dragon paperweight
returned

everyone has a theory
of who took the dragon and why

but *han* six is quiet
too quiet, until Yuki
tells the teacher
she saw me take it

she offers a story about how
I thought it was cool
that since learning that this school
was once called Dragon's Mouth
I wanted that paperweight
and she thinks it's in my house
and why doesn't the teacher *just go check?*

Ōshima-sensei doesn't
disagree or agree but says
he knows that if I took it
I will certainly return it

the whole class
then seems convinced
that I have done something
with the missing dragon

I'm so glad to get to aikido on Thursday
so glad to see Yamada-sensei
who makes everyone respect each other
who's strict but fun, and whose way
makes everyone cooperate

at the end of the class
I linger a little
talking and joking
with the assistant teacher

then I ride beside another
orange belt, Manabu
and his sister Nana
as they walk home

then I take my time along
the river, listening for fish
watching them jump
before riding home

that night
I tell Cora
about the dragon paperweight
and how Yuki accused me

and Cora says
don't worry
Yuki doesn't have evidence
so Ōshima-sensei won't believe her

but being accused
by someone in your *han*
is bigger than just a matter
of evidence

and it takes me ages
to fall asleep

Chapter 28

INTRUDER

when I wake in the night
I think it's Mom or Dad
standing in our room
backlit by streetlight
dimmed by thin curtains
but then I see that actually it's someone . . .
             shorter?

I jerk my head up
something clanks onto
the desk and I yell
and Cora shrieks
as the intruder
runs out of our room

I race after
whoever it is
    down the stairs
        out the front door
            and as he disappears
                down our street
            and turns the corner
                into the bath of streetlight

I see the side of his face

and I shout at Gō
to *stop!*

Dad reaches the front steps behind me
what the hell's going on?

I tell him *some guy was in our house*

did you see him?

not really I say

did he take anything?

I don't know I say

and I go back inside
run upstairs
past Mom and Dad's room
where Cora's crying
and Mom is holding her
into Cora's and my room
where I see that it's
not something taken
but something left

on my desk
the dragon paperweight

how'd the guy get in?
Dad's shouting from the hall
I locked the door before
I went to bed!

and right then I know

that someone

Shō, Ken, or Yōhei—
      the only friends who've
      ever been with me
      when I forgot my house key
      the only friends who've
      ever seen me get the spare key
      from a jar under a clay pot
      that we keep near our bicycles
must have told Gō

I shove the dragon paperweight
under my pillow
before anyone can see
and then I go
into the other room
and ask Cora
did you recognize him?

Mom has her back to me
and Cora sees me
just barely shake my head
to mean *no*

no Cora says
but Mom whips around
and narrows her eyes
at me

did YOU see? Mom asks me
did YOU recognize him?

I don't want to lie
but right now I can't
tell the truth

I didn't get a good look I say
he was backlit and he ran
as soon as I woke up

when Cora's settled
back in her bunk
and Mom and Dad
have locked all the doors
and windows

I climb down the bunk ladder
and scoot in next to Cora

it was that boy from your class! she whispers
the one who was with the boy
on the lightning bike at the temple!

yeah I say
but don't tell for now

why not?
what will you do?
you HAVE to tell!

no I say
just give me some time
so I can figure this out

Chapter 29

HEAD DOWN

Dad discovers
the spare key is missing
and assumes that someone
was watching one day
when I retrieved it

so now until we change the lock
we have another secret hiding place
that I can't tell or show
anyone

and Cora and I have to always
keep our keys with us

when Cora and I leave for school
Mom and Dad are gulping coffee
waiting for the police

should I stay home? I ask
but they say no, they'll share
the general details I gave

go on to school Dad says
keep your head up
don't worry about this

hah!

he doesn't seem to get
that my head is a target
smacked every day

that keeping your head *down*
is the way to survive
in the Dragon's Mouth

at school I go straight
to the teacher's room
on the ground floor and ask
to speak with Ōshima-sensei

I hand over the dragon paperweight
and tell him Yuki was right
it was at my house and I bow
apologizing for the trouble I've caused

Ōshima-sensei frowns
and chews on his lips
as he cradles the dragon
with two hands

he eyes me
shakes his head
like maybe he's
disappointed

but I don't know if he's disappointed
because he thinks I took it
or disappointed because he knows
I'm covering for the person who really took it

upstairs in our classroom
I don't say anything
don't look at Gō or Yuki
just keep a blank face

Ōshima-sensei tells the class
that the dragon paperweight was found
and everyone waits to hear more
but he doesn't say how or where

he wants our attention
on classwork now
the dragon paperweight case
is closed

han six seems puzzled
but I just focus on *kanji*
then on math
and art

no one hits me
no one bothers me
but tension builds
all day

at the end of school
Ōshima-sensei tells Yuki and Gō
to stay after

then unlike usual, Yōhei
doesn't walk home
with Ken, Shō, and me

on the way, Ken and Shō analyze
the situation, thinking Yuki and Gō
are the ones responsible

I don't tell them
I handed in the dragon paperweight
I don't say I know that Gō
broke into our house
I don't say I know he did it
with help from my "friends"

but outside my house
I duck my head
tell them

> *I can't play soccer today*

Chapter 30

DRAGON WEIGHT

Dad is still at home
and he says they talked
with police and the principal
and my teacher and they think
it's probably someone from school . . .
can we talk later? I have to play soccer
I say, and drop my bag and run out the door

I ride my bike toward Takemura's
then detour to a convenience store
for a bag of chips so at least
I'll have something
to pass as a "gift"

Takemura-san's there
and he motions me in
with his hand even though
his face is scowling

we set up the *shōgi* board
and when he asks about Cora
I say she's playing with a friend
even though this might not be true

we start to play and I try
but I can't focus on the grid
even though his advice
on moves is clear enough

then I catch his words saying
that my mood seems heavy

     I'm tired I admit

     then after a moment, I add
     and I'm kind of hiding out

I catch the word *mugicha*—barley tea
and following his waving
go into the kitchen
and in the refrigerator find a pitcher
take two cups from a cupboard
and pour us each some chilled tea

I set his cup on the *shōgi* table
gulp mine down
then realize I have to
pick up the cup
guide the cup
into his hand

he's shakier
today

I notice he's watching
waiting for me to speak

so I tell him what happened
with the dragon paperweight
and how I thought my *han*
members would be protected
if I didn't turn them in
which would mean that I'd
then be protected by the *han*
and they'd stop bothering me
but now I think somehow
they've been found out
and my plan totally failed

also, I don't think
the matter is solved at all
just because the dragon
has been returned

Takemura-san then starts right in
telling the old dragon story
but he's halting, so it's mostly me
filling in with my mind
where his words are slurred
or me filling in out loud
when he's stuck for words

it's the story that I know
from teachers, neighbors, kids
and from Dad who loves local history and legends

the story about the dragon
who was always eating children
snacking on them a few at a time
and the Benten goddess on the island
he fell in love with who persuaded him
to finally stop his destructive munching ways

and about how, after he stopped
feeling badly for all he'd done
he turned himself into a mountain
the place called Dragon's Mouth
the place right here
where we live

Takemura-san says
(more or less)
you see?
even dragons
can change

hah! I think

maybe in stories I say

I open the bag
and we eat the chips
then I say good-bye

promising to bring Cora
with me next time

but when I step outside
when I close the gate
to Takemura's house
I see that my bike

is not by the river wall
where I left it

and is not anywhere
in sight at all

Chapter 31

BIKE TRADE

I walk up and down
side lanes by the river
check paths along the banks
walk both sides of the bridge
and even stare down
into the murky water

I've gone halfway
to the police box
thinking to report
my missing bike
when I double back
with one last idea

that last idea
for where I might find my bike
being across the bridge
near Takemura's

I search the shrubs
edging the pine tree park
where Shunta took us
that day to watch the fire

and there it is, still locked
standing upright
leaning on its kickstand
like I'd parked it there myself

I feel watched
        as I fit my key in the lock
I feel spied on
        as I kick up the stand
I try to act cool
        as I ride away from the park

I decide to take the long way home
the back road that meanders
beyond the monorail
across the town line

but as I'm cutting over to that route
past the station's rear parking lot
I glimpse the familiar flames
and lightning bolts of Shunta's bike

I pedal past
telling myself
>   *be cool*
>   *be smart*
>   *ride on*

but I can't help myself

I make a U-turn

I don't carry his bike far

just to a small alley
two houses down
from the parking lot

then I pedal fast
out of that neighborhood
across the city line

on the way I stop to call home
and Cora answers
says Yūsuke just left
and that she got to have
my tutoring session
Mom gets on the phone
and says I'm in hot
hot water

I zigzag
through back lanes
and climb up the far
shoulder side
of the dragon hill

avoiding
the school
the park
the neighborhoods
by the streetcar

taking the long, safe way
to our house

I'm so late
that Mom's yelling
when I open the front door
but she stops

when I tell her
about my temporarily
missing bike
now found

I don't tell her
about the other temporarily
        missing bike

        found by now?

during dinner I learn that the police
questioned Mom further about the night intruder
and seem to believe it's a kid from my school
but to Mom's interrogation about who it might be
I insist I have no idea

I take an extra-long bath
wondering if

>moving Shunta's bike
>was like
>an aikido strike—*uchi*

or if

>moving Shunta's bike
>was like
>a defensive throw—*nage*

and I'm wondering
if I'll have to quit school
like Daiki did

if I'll have to
stay home
and never go out

later Cora climbs up to my bunk
and even though I turn to the wall
and tell her I don't want to talk
she says she has our Gray agenda
all planned for the weekend

whatever it is I say
it better be
> *far away*
> *on the other side of town*
> *or in another city*
> *or prefecture*
> *or country*
> *or universe*

oh she says
and climbs down

then something lands on my back—
one of Gray's friends
a stuffed raccoon
tossed up for me

Chapter 32

GAMES AND PLAY DAY

it's just my luck that Sunday
is the annual Games and Play Day
and we have to go to school

Mom and Dad are both volunteers
Dad at the stilts area outside
Mom on slime making inside

I figure with all the parents
there at school
nothing major can happen to me

hah!

fortunately in the bowling room
han six is in charge with
han two which is Ken's *han*
so I can mostly hang with him
and not get too close
to anyone from *han* six

but Shunta and Gō
maneuver around
and attempt to trip me
or slam me into the wall
and throw tennis balls
and plastic bottles at my head

Ken inserts himself
between me and them
again and again
and some other kids
join to protect me
like it's a big game

when our shift is over
I go outside to help Dad
        but even there Shunta and Gō
        follow like shadows

all polite to my Dad
Shunta and Gō ask
if I can play with them
have some fun and make some
slime together

Dad thinks it's friendly and innocent
says *sure, go ahead!* and even though I resist
he urges me to join them so finally
instead of making a scene
I do

as soon as we're out of Dad's sight
they put me in a headlock
and Shunta's smiling so that
parents and teachers we pass
think he's just fooling around

     but under his breath
     he's cursing

Gō grabs one of my fingers
pulls it back till it's about to break
and makes me walk with them
to the school chicken coop

and behind the coop Shunta snarls
you told on us, you jerk!
you said Gō took the dragon
and you touched my bicycle!
he spits in my face

I start to deny that I ever
said anything about Gō
but Shunta smacks me so fast
and so hard
I fall backward
bite my tongue
and taste blood

fortunately Ken
rounds the corner of the coop
stares them down
helps me get up
and walks with me
back to the school ground

Ken has the bright idea
to tell my parents I'm feeling sick
and offers to walk me home

on the way he says
everyone knows
you didn't take the dragon
even Ōshima-sensei!
everyone knows
Gō was involved!
so don't let them get you alone
stay with me and Yōhei and Shō
at school, we'll guard you
even when you walk home
we'll guard you, and eventually
they'll just forget about all this

he's trying hard
but I'm thinking
> Yōhei betrayed me
> he told Gō
> where we hid the key

> so who will be next?

at home
when Ken leaves
I lock the front door
lock all the windows
thinking of Daiki
locking his garden gate

I climb up into my bunk
and when Mom, Dad, and Cora return
I don't have to work hard
to act sick

Chapter 33

SUSPICION

Monday is a comp day
we have no school
so I can stay home
all day indoors
and do mindless stuff—

check the Shōnan Gray spreadsheet
help Cora choose the best photos
for our first set of clear folders
search prices for printing
and help Cora design a logo

I don't leave the house
until I get into the car
for the ride to English group

at English group
we share updates on our projects
divide into olders and youngers
and study more about business

and I report
and participate
but all afternoon
I'm half listening
just saying words
acting fine
but I'm not

because I suspect
Shunta and Gō
and all of *han* six
have a fight
in mind

on Tuesday
han six is watching me
      my every twitch or squirm
      my every mark in every workbook
      my every stroke in every *kanji*

now Ōshima-sensei
is also watching *han* six
at last

but when Ōshima-sensei
leaves the room
Shunta leans close
grabs my shirt, says
      what'd you tell him?

I don't answer
I don't defend myself
I don't even say
that I didn't say anything
because I know
it doesn't matter

all that ever matters
is what Shunta thinks

after school I ask my tutor Yūsuke
if he ever got into fights
and how he saved himself
but he dodges the question
then says mostly he got beat up
because he did stupid things
to kids who could fight well
like trip them or throw rocks

after he leaves
I fill two large
plastic bottles
with water

and up in my room
after push-ups
and sit-ups
and aikido exercises
I lift those bottles
like barbells
while holding firm

       my center

Chapter 34

BREATH

on Wednesday
Shunta and Gō
with the rest of *han* six
tell me at lunchtime
meet us after school
at the gate to
Dragon's Mouth Temple

I tell them I watch Cora
on Wednesdays

they shrug, say
you better be there

I tell Ken and Shō
and they walk
on either side of me
to the after-school center

don't meet them they say
keep away from them they say
that's the best way
then they leave for *juku*

and I wonder if
what they say is true
or if hiding will just make
everything worse

I find Cora in the garden
decorating *dango*
and this time I don't rush her
I let her take all the time she needs
to adorn her mud balls

finally she's the one
who's first to say *I'm ready*

she's the one
who twice repeats
come on, J, let's go

and I almost argue
almost start making
my own *dango*
with decorations
of grass and leaves
and flowers
just to stall

but I take a deep breath
sign her out from the center
and we put on our shoes

when we slide back the door
we see them waiting
Shunta, Gō, Naho, Yuki
and no Mika
but Yōhei

Gō says
we thought you might be thinking
of trying to escape

Cora eyes me, eyes them
pulls on my arm
says in English
let's go back inside

but I say quietly
we have to go along
just for a bit
then we'll get away
have an adventure

and Cora says
I don't care about an adventure
I want to go home

but we don't go home

we walk down the road
past the school
Cora by my side
Shunta and Gō in front
Naho, Yuki
and Yōhei
trailing behind

Shunta and Gō are arguing
and I'm keeping an eye out
for some hero to come along
or some distraction to appear
as they lead us toward
Dragon's Mouth Temple
by the curve in the streetcar tracks

but no handy heroes arrive
and we all step through the first gate
between guardian deva kings
with their bulging glass eyes
        ready to do battle
        against evil

we climb stone steps
to the second gate
cross the temple grounds
climb more steps and cut left
at the incense urn

we edge the huge main hall
and climb rear stone stairs
to the sub-shrine with the guardian deity
that also has something to do with a dragon
but I can't remember what

we hike through woods to the place
where there's a break in the chain-link fence
along the temple land boundary
and Cora grips my hand tight
as I help her through the gap

we follow the narrow path
that leads to a small park where
Cora used to play with her preschool—
and we walk until Shunta
stops, says *here*

here what? I say

here's where we do it

do what? I ask

and Shunta smirks
play
it's fun
but first
send your sister away

Cora grabs my arm

she can stay I say
she likes fun

no Shunta says
no little kids

I say *let me talk to her*

thinking of aikido
        calm and action
        as one

Cora starts to whine
and I switch to English
say *listen to me and do exactly*
what I tell you to do

and even though the others can't
understand most of my words
I know they know the word "help"
and I know they're watching
my every move so I tell her
you have to go now
but let's do some
multiplication first

multiplication? she says
are you crazy?

no, I'm serious I say
I'll pretend I'm mad at you
and you have to pretend
you're mad at me, got it?

I'm raising my voice now
and finally
Cora's listening

and it's simple
but I can't think of anything else

so I speak in English like I'm mad
just answer: what's 3×3?

nine! she says and stomps like she's furious
but it's a stomp I know as acting

what's 10×10−99? I say
she sneers and says *one!*

then before I can say another problem
she says *so, what's 7×1÷7?*

one! I say and add
now get out of here!

she spins around and over her shoulder
hollers in English *I hate you, Jason Parker!*
then calls me and the others
all the Japanese curse words she knows
and runs off through the break in the fence
and into the woods
                    out of sight

whether she gets help
or not
it's better
without her
I'm not distracted
I'm centered
and focused
ready to fight
ten million men

but Shunta laughs
on seeing my ready posture
says *no, we have something*
more interesting planned
so we can welcome you
into the group

Yōhei says a few words to Shunta
trying to get him to give it up
that you don't *make* someone play it
that it's everyone's choice to do it

whatever "it" is

but Shunta yells at Yōhei
and Gō suddenly smacks him
and Yōhei is so unprepared
he stumbles partway down
        an embankment
                into a tree

and in that moment
when Yōhei is smacked
I've lost my focus
and my center
and Shunta
tries to
shove me

I catch his arm
and manage a wrist lock
turn him
yank him off balance
and now he's mad

but it's rough, uneven ground
sloping off on both sides
so I can't find my footing
to center myself
and Shunta then hurls
all his weight at me
and I fall back

soon he's kneeling
on my chest
and I'm trying to fight him off
but he's yelling at me
and hitting me
and I'm fighting
and struggling
and he's heavy
on my chest

then Gō
is helping him hold me down

and Shunta says
do it

not if he doesn't want to! Gō says

do it! Shunta orders

and Gō reaches for my neck
not strangling but
pressing on the sides
and Shunta kneels
harder on my chest
while pinning my arms

until I have no fight
and no breath

and the sound of the grove
and of Yōhei yelling
and Naho . . . crying?
and the twigs snapping
and bamboo grass
slipping

beneath me
disappear

Chapter 35

CORA

evidently

Cora does
get help

the monk
tending the amulet
and incense sales
inside the main hall
of the temple

and she doesn't stop there

when she leads the monk
up the hill and through the fence break
and they find

me
unmoving

and the others
shaking
and slapping

me
unresponsive

she calls emergency
she calls Mom
she calls Dad
she calls emergency again
tells them to *hurry!*
then stays right by

me
unconscious

they say Cora told Shunta
she'd kill him if I died

they say it was the monk's
immediate resuscitation efforts that saved me

they say Cora stayed right by me
talking at me nonstop

they say the ambulance didn't arrive
until well after I'd regained consciousness

they say that Cora cursed at me
when my eyes started closing again

and they say that not until I was alert
and taking water at the hospital
and Mom had arrived
did Cora let herself cry
and let go of my arm

now moving

Chapter 36

ACHES

I stay overnight
at the hospital

Dad stays with me
sleeping in a chair

Mom takes Cora home

at the hospital
the next day
they do X-rays
and test after test

Cora and Mom bring
cups of custard pudding
that slides nice and easy
down my throat

and we wait
for results

but other than a cracked rib
and a throbbing headache
and cuts and scrapes and bruises
I seem to be okay

and they let me go home
in the evening

Cora and I
Mom and Dad
we all
take the rest of the week
off

and finally I speak
about everything
that has happened
     in the classroom
     on the seawall
     near Daiki's house
     by Takemura's
     after school

and I ask Cora again
what happened up on the hill
in the woods above
Dragon's Mouth Temple

she explains
second by second
step by step
after-school center
to hill
to hospital
but I still wonder
one thing

I know she caught
my 911 code
which is opposite
of Japan's 119

I know she knew
to get help right away
but I wonder
>how did she know
>to get help that fast
>especially when Shunta said
>he just wanted to play?

duh! she says
because I could hear them talking
about chissoku

chissoku? I ask

choking! she says

when were they talking
about choking?

on the way to the temple
and up on the hill she says
Yōhei and Naho were arguing
Naho saying it'd be okay
because Shunta had done it to Gō
and Gō had done it to Shunta
and they were perfectly fine . . .
they wanted to make you play
the choking game

I realize
I'd been looking out
for someone to save me
during the walk
and listening so closely
to Shunta and Gō
on the hill
watching their moves
thinking of my moves
preparing to fight
an army of ten million men

that I'd missed this
major clue

choking game?

I can't help but shiver
and my mom
wraps a fleece blanket
around me

until I have to run
to the toilet

to throw up

my parents talk
to the police
Cora talks to the police
and when I'm feeling better
late on Friday
I also talk to the police
       Nakazato-san—
              the officer we spoke to about the sandal
       plus one other man

I can't answer all their questions
and some of the words I don't know
but they won't let Dad translate
which makes Dad blow up
so the questioning is halted
and Dad gets on his phone
hunting down legal support

we have visits from the principal
        vice principal
        head of the PTA
        class parent leaders
        Ōshima-sensei
who all promise change
in slightly different versions

and on Saturday
we drive to Yokohama
to meet with a counselor

we talk and talk
on and on
        straight
        through
        the
        weekend

then late Sunday afternoon
the doorbell rings again and
Ken and Shō are on our steps
with Yōhei hiding behind them

why's he here? I ask

Yōhei hangs back
but Ken and Shō pull him
up the steps
and into our house

we sit in the living room
the three of them stiffly on the sofa
me at the edge of a chair
with Cora perched on its arm

Mom brings cups of tea
some rice crackers
sets them on the coffee table
but no one touches a thing

Mom and Dad
hover in the doorway

I sit on the chair
stone still

and Ken and Shō
nudge Yōhei

who presses his lips together
inhales
like he's going under water
then exhales
a blast of apologies

     for not being a friend
     for telling Gō about the spare key
     for not being able to stop Shunta and Gō

not being able to stop them? I say
you knew what they were planning!
you and Naho talked about it!
you went along with it!

and I don't care
how my Japanese sounds—
smart, stupid, babyish, formal
I can't stop yelling at him

and then he's crying
and Mom is next to him
offering tissues

why didn't you help me? I say

Yōhei covers his face
and says *I tried!*
I called 119—
even before your sister
came back

I stand up
but you let them attack me!
you didn't even warn me!

it wasn't an attack Yōhei says
it was a kind of game

Shunta pushed me down! I say
Shunta held me down!
Gō cut off my breath
that's an attack!

Yōhei uncovers his face and says
I tried to stop them!
I thought I could divert them
I was trying to make them quit
that choking game thing
I went in case they did too much . . .

then my father's in the room
and his voice booms

      too much?
      just when were you going to figure out
      that ALL of this was too much?
      when our son was dead?
      choking is never a GAME!

next thing my mother's ushering my father out of the room
saying that we need to continue this discussion
at another time, when their parents are here
when we can have someone professional here
someone to assist us, someone to mediate

but I call Dad back into the room

tell the story I say
that one about the white deer
and the French guy

he objects
doesn't see the point right now
but I insist

no he says—
that story is "fakelore"
recorded by a Brooklyn man
not a Native storyteller

just tell it! I say

and so he sits down
heavily on the floor
closes his eyes
and tells it
in Japanese this time
a little changed and halting
but it's mostly the same
and Yōhei quiets
and everyone's still

I make Dad tell the story to the end
then ask him to go back to retell
the part where that one tribe member
brings the white deer to the Frenchman
who kills it and takes the skin

and I say to Yōhei
     you
you were like that member of the tribe
who sold the white deer
we were good friends
we were like a tribe
the four of us
but you . . .

uragiru is the word Dad used
and I can see the characters now
裏切る—literally, to backstab
and I try that word now in Japanese

you betrayed me

and that aches more
than my cracked rib

Chapter 37

SEAT CHANGE

I don't have to
but I do
I return to school
to the Dragon's Mouth

I can leave
when I want
switch to international school
when I want
Mom and Dad will find the money
somehow, they've said

but I'm thinking
I've worked hard
to read and write
Japanese

and I'm thinking
I have the right to graduate
with my sixth-grade class
in March

and I'm thinking
maybe I can start
to make things change
for others

Shunta and Gō
have been suspended
so when I return to school
on the Tuesday after

han six is me
plus three girls
who avoid
meeting my eyes

and the first
order of business
is seat change

but this time we don't
draw slips of paper
this time Ōshima-sensei
calls out our names
and tells us where to sit
and this time
all six members
of *han* six
are split up

finally Ōshima-sensei talks about bullying
that it's not just groups against one person
but also one or two against one person
and that three types of bullying are
 verbal
 social
 physical
and that all three were used in our class
plus
 damage of property

he says we all
need to reflect
and improve

he says
think about whether
or when you have been
 bully
 victim
 or bystander

still there is no talk of
rules for
        no hitting
        or hands off

but school is basically calm

like a normal school day
should be

Cora and I go to Daiki's
on Wednesday
to start his English lessons
so he can move to Hawaii

he thinks I'm crazy to keep going
to my school but I tell him
that we reminded teachers, the PTA
even the police of his situation

I tell him we told them
that too many people
in the school, including adults
have been bystanders of bullying

I tell him the town is in the spotlight
and things have to change

Daiki says *right*
wait till those two guys
are back in school
then see how you feel

I tell him I'll let him know

then we get started on English
and discover he's been studying
plenty while he's on his own

and actually is pretty good

Cora and I try to help him sound more natural
help him put words he knows into sentences
help him talk less like a teacher or textbook

we both want things
to be easier for him
in his school in Hawaii

we both know
what it's like
not to have enough words

and we all know
it's hard enough
just being different

then near the end of our "lesson" Daiki says
you both study in an English group, right?
do you think I could go, too?

and after that, on Mondays
Mom picks up Cora and me
and then Daiki
to go to English group

and Daiki doesn't understand
all our words
but he learns fast
starts to trust the group
and likes how the olders
just accept him
no big deal
and how the youngers
act like he's some
really cool
older brother

one day
and another go by

and inside the Dragon's Mouth
my head is not smacked
and my body is not slammed

and I feel like I can ride my bike
through any neighborhood
again

I can't do aikido
until my rib is healed
which is after the
demonstration day
I'd practiced so hard for

but I visit the dojo
and Yamada-sensei
makes me promise
to consult him if I ever
have problems again

he says aikido
is not a superpower
I should never think
I'm some superhero
just because I do aikido

he says we need to train
so that we sense danger
                in order to avoid it

as we talk, kneeling in the dojo
all quiet before the students arrive
he says aikido is not
just to defend against attackers
but also to defend against stress
that aikido is training of body and mind
finding harmony and forgiveness

the world is full of all kinds of people
and some of them are a bit lost he says
but keep in mind the saying
          'sow good and the harvest will be good'

he looks at me
          we have to try he says

Yamada-sensei asks me
if I want to continue my training

and I say I do

he asks if I'd like to help
with the beginner classes
while I'm healing
and maybe even after

and I bow
as far as my cracked rib
allows

because of course
I do

Chapter 38

REFLECTION

before Shunta and Gō
return to school

there are PTA meetings
and meetings of class parents
and meetings between Mom and Dad
and all the parents of former *han* six

and as Mom and Dad say
things might not change overnight
but at least people are now talking
and at least some are listening
and at least some are taking action

when I visit Takemura-san
to deliver a box of brownies
in thanks for the kite
that he and his daughter sent me
when they heard the news

he says he wants to go out for a walk

I'm not so sure about this
since he shuffles and gets stuck
and doesn't seem very steady today

but I agree
and slowly
slowly
we go down the path
    and cross the bridge
        stopping to watch
            a fish leaping
                upriver

it's a warm day for November
and the river, the trees
the air barely move

at the tilted pine park
we sit down on a bench
then I run to a vending machine
at the far end of the park
insert two coins and buy us each
      a cool can of oolong tea

Takemura-san shuts his eyes
gulps and sighs
and when he's done he thanks me
while tremors make his left leg
and the whole bench
      jiggle

he gestures with his arm
to the river, the trees
toward the port and bay
this . . . he says *is a good place* . . .
      peaceful

and it's true
when you don't have to
fear someone like Shunta
and his followers
      it is a good, peaceful place

when Shunta and Gō
do return to school
under some kind of probation
ordered by family court

I keep my distance

and they keep theirs

Ōshima-sensei watches them closely
a teaching aide watches them closely
everyone watches them closely
still wary of what they might do

a counseling group
visits our school
to help resolve the situation
Ōshima-sensei says

there's a grade six conference
and a smaller special session
with members of former *han* six
plus Yōhei, Shō, Ken, and kids
who have been my friends
            even Satomi

we talk about incidents
and what happened
and we're supposed to share
how we feel now
and how we felt then

but no one in class
wants to say too much
no one wants to rat
on anyone else
no one yet trusts
they won't be a target
in the future
if they say too much

the counselors ask us
to write down our ideas
but it's hard for me
to write these thoughts
especially in Japanese
and especially
when the problems
seem so obvious

I just want to move on
have nothing to do with
Shunta
Gō
Naho
Yuki
and Mika

but the counselor
asks me please
to write

and I remember some words
of my aikido sensei
        about a calm mind
        being reflected in others

and so I write
and then I share
what I wrote

which is basically

that I want it to be okay to be different
that I don't want any hitting allowed
that words from teachers *are* enough
        they don't need to hit students
that I don't want kids to just watch
        when something's wrong
that I want our school to teach respect
that I think everyone, and I mean

everyone
        should learn
                aikido

Chapter 39

IN THE DRAGON'S MOUTH

that last point of which
was maybe a mistake
since now that I'm helping
with the beginner class

when Shunta shows up
at the dojo a few weeks later
in his brand new
stiff white *gi*

    word having gotten
    to family court
    what I said about aikido

I have to teach him

Yamada-sensei knows
exactly who Shunta is
in relation to me

but he keeps saying
whenever Shunta's not certain
about how to tie his belt
or the posture for the *ki* breathing
or how to tuck for the back rolls
or how to position his thumb for a hold

to watch or listen
to Pākā-*kun*

which is me
Parker
as in Jason Parker

not my first name
but my last name
for respect

at the end of his first class
Shunta's there in the entryway
listening to the teacher
as I step out of the changing room

I hear Yamada-sensei tell Shunta—
    Mori-*kun* he calls him
    using his last name
that if he trains well
he might get his green belt
in a few months

I can see Shunta's embarrassed
like I was
back when I was white belt

it seems like forever
until the first test
and the green belt

I hang back in a corner
fiddle with stuff in my bag
wait till Shunta's gone
to leave the dojo

but when I step outside
Shunta's still there
where the bikes are parked

talking with another kid
yellow belt
someone he knows

I almost turn around
and go back inside
to hide

but maybe because
I've just come from
the calm of the dojo
or maybe because I know
Yamada-sensei's right inside

I find myself
going over to my bike
which is right by Shunta's

unlocking my bike
while he's straddling his
      with the lightning bolts
      and darting flames

then saying
smoothly

you know
you should start a business
custom painting bicycles

and I'm surprised
by my words
and Shunta's surprised
by my words

and I think
for a moment
he's going to
throw a punch

like
maybe he's thinking
*what would you know
about anything*?

but instead
he shakes his head
and holds up a hand
the way you're supposed to
when you're complimented

denying it
ducking a bit
implying you're no good

but I know
he knows
he's good

I get on my bike

and maybe because
Yamada-sensei comes out
to stand on the steps
and says I'm doing well
teaching the beginners
and once my rib is
fully healed I can
take the test
for my blue belt

or maybe because
as I start to ride off
a fish jumps three times
then twice more
slapping the water
leaving a trail of rings

or maybe just because
my little sister
saved my life

I shout to Shunta
over my shoulder
as I pedal away

I'm good with numbers
if you need an accountant

or a boss, I think
      if painting bicycles should happen
      to turn into a business

hah!

and I ride on home
here
in the Dragon's Mouth

GLOSSARY

Pronunciation Guide

Japanese has only five basic vowel sounds, *a, i, u, e, o*: *a* as in "taco"; *i* as in "ski"; *u* as in "uber"; *e* as in "egg"; *o* as in "oat." Vowels are short unless marked with a macron indicating a long sound. The *r* is slightly rolled. The *g* is hard as in "get." Pronunciation of each syllable is quite even and unaccented.

aikidō aikido; Japanese martial art of harmonizing life energy for self defense

baka idiot, jerk, fool

bōken adventure

bōya boy

bunchin paperweight

chissoku choking, suffocation

dagashi Japanese-style penny candy

dango round dumpling made of *mochi* rice flour

doro dango mud or dirt ball

dōjō dojo; a school or practice hall for training in martial arts

dōzo please come in

genkan entryway

gi uniform for aikido (or other martial arts) training

gyōza Japanese-style pan-fried Chinese dumplings

hāfu half, a term for biracial people in Japan

hai yes

han group or team

hisha flying chariot in the game of *shōgi*

hōjicha a kind of green tea that is roasted to a brown color

irasshaimase shopkeeper's welcome

iyada no way, not a chance

judō judo; a competitive Japanese martial art involving throws or takedowns

juku cram school

kanji Chinese characters used in Japanese writing

kawaī cute

ken right, authority

kendō kendo; Japanese martial art that uses bamboo swords

ki 氣 or 気 life force or life energy, a central focus of aikido

koma playing pieces in the game of *shōgi*

kun name suffix for a boy, as in Mori-*kun*

mada not yet

mikan Japanese mandarin orange

mochi glutinous rice

mugicha barley tea, often served chilled

nage a throw in aikido

nā a word/sentence ending for emphasis

nō brain, mind

oi hey!

ōshō king in the game of *shōgi*

ryū dragon

ryūma dragon horse in the game of *shōgi*

sābisu from the English word "service," meaning on the
house

san name suffix, polite, as in Takemura-san

sensei teacher, teacher of martial arts

shōgi Japanese chess-like game

Shōnan coastal region in Japan's Kanagawa Prefecture
along Sagami Bay

sugoi or *sugei* (slang) cool, amazing, great, impressive,
wow!

tatami a mat made of woven straw that is stretched over
a filling and used as flooring in a traditional

Japanese house or room; each mat is a standard size, and room sizes are described in *tatami* units (a six-mat room, an eight-mat room, etc.)

uchi a strike in aikido

unchi poop

uragiru to betray, to turn traitor

yakitori grilled chicken on skewers

CULTURAL GUIDE

Japanese elementary schools cover grades one to six. The Japanese school year begins in April and ends in March, and consists of three terms (April–July, September–December, January–March) with a six-week summer break and shorter winter and spring breaks. Students change into indoor shoes when they enter a school. Students in public elementary schools generally do not wear uniforms, and class size may be up to about thirty-five students. Students take part in school cleaning duties and hold other assigned roles of responsibility. In the classroom, students are often organized in *han,* or groups.

Juku are Japanese "cram" schools or after-school schools. Many students, like Jason's friends Yōhei, Shō, and Ken, attend *juku* several times per week from elementary through high school, in addition to attending public or private school, in order to gain skills necessary to pass rigorous entrance exams for middle schools, high schools, or universities.

The Japanese writing system consists of *kanji* derived from Chinese characters plus two phonetic syllabaries: *hiragana* and *katakana*. There are about two thousand commonly used *kanji,* about one thousand of which are taught in elementary school. In grade six, Jason's grade, students learn about 180 new *kanji* during the school year plus many compounds (combinations of *kanji* to create different meanings or words).

Japanese houses and apartments come in different styles, but all have some sort of *genkan* or entryway where shoes are removed before stepping up into the living area. Some homes are more traditionally Japanese in style, with a room or rooms that have *tatami*-mat flooring, sliding interior doors, and large closets for stowing folding futons.

Baths are a daily evening ritual in Japan, and Japanese homes usually have a dedicated bathing room that is separate from the toilet room. Tubs are deep. Washing is done outside the bath before entering the tub for soaking.

Aikido is a Japanese martial art that means the way of harmonizing or unifying life energy or *ki*. Aikido involves turning and redirecting an attacker's energy and requires physical and mental training. Jason practices *Shinshin Toitsu* Aikido, also known as *Ki* Aikido.

Doro dango are small spheres made of dirt or sand and water, often created in sandboxes at playgrounds and schools. If patiently polished, *doro dango* may acquire a shiny surface.

Dragons are important mythological creatures throughout Asia. In Japan, dragons are associated with rain, clouds, and water and figure prominently in Buddhism. Many Japanese temples feature ceiling paintings of dragons, or *ryū*. Jason's Kamakura neighborhood is rich with dragon lore.

Insects are commonly collected and kept in terrariums or carrying cages in Japan. Jason's tutor, Yūsuke, gives Jason a bell cricket, or *suzumushi*, to keep.

Kamakura is a seaside city in Kanagawa Prefecture along the Shōnan Coast, about thirty miles (fifty kilometers) southwest of Tōkyō. From roughly 1185 until 1333, Kamakura was the military capital of Japan, and the city today is rich with historical sites including many ancient temples and shrines and samurai cave tombs. Jason's story takes place in Kamakura and surrounding areas. Manpukuji is the temple famous for the Koshigoe letter said to have been written by Minamoto no Yoshitsune; the Great Buddha is one of the most famous Buddha statues in Japan; Engakuji, where the white deer are said to have appeared, is one of the most prominent Zen temples in Japan; and the Enoden streetcar that connects Kamakura with the city of Fujisawa runs through Jason's neighborhood. Along the Kamakura city border with Fujisawa lies Ryūkōji (Dragon's Mouth Temple). This temple and the nearby island of Enoshima, with its Benten Shrine and dragon cave, are featured in the dragon tale that Takemura-san tells.

Police boxes known as *kōban* are small neighborhood police stations that operate in addition to the larger police stations. Neighborhood policing practices include officers introducing themselves to new residents and learning family names and businesses in a neighborhood.

Japanese foods are wide-ranging. Rice or noodles are featured at most meals. Foods mentioned in this story include *yakitori*—grilled chicken morsels on skewers; *gyōza*—a Japanese version of a Chinese dumpling; *dagashi* sweets—a Japanese style of penny candy; green and purple ice cream—soft-serve made with green tea ice cream and purple sweet potato ice cream; *mochi*—glutinous rice often used to make sweets, including *dango*; and rice crackers, which are a common snack.

Japanese teas include many varieties of green tea, including *hōjicha,* a roasted tea that Daiki serves to Jason and Cora. Also common is *mugicha*, barley tea, and oolong tea, both of which are especially refreshing when served chilled.

Name order in Japan is family name followed by given name, so when Daiki introduces himself he says, "Nakano Daiki," with Nakano being his family name. Children usually go by their given names in elementary school. Takemura is a family name, as are Ōshima and Yamada.

Typhoons are tropical cyclones (like hurricanes) that occur in the northwest Pacific Ocean. Typhoons are common in Japan from July through October.

Tora-san is the beloved character played by Kiyoshi Atsumi in the forty-eight films of the series *Otoko wa tsurai yo* (It's Tough Being a Man). Each film features a different region of Japan and a different leading woman (with some repeating).

Shōgi is a Japanese game similar to chess played on a grid by two opponents with twenty playing pieces each. Captured pieces may be put back into play.

RESOURCES

Stop Bullying (U.S. Dept. of Health and Human Services website): stopbullying.gov

Erik's Cause (dialogue and resources to combat "the choking game"): erikscause.org

Kids Web Japan (Ministry of Foreign Affairs, Japan): web -japan.org/kidsweb/

Ki Aikido Documentary (documentary produced in Brazil shared via London Ki Aikido): londonkiaikido.wordpress .com/2013/05/31/ki-aikido-documentary/

Shinshin Toitsu Aikido (Ki Aikido information): shinshin toitsuaikido.org/english/

Austin Ki Aikido Center (Ki Aikido sample class information): akac.org/your-first-class/

Economics Education Web (lessons such as those taught in Jason's English group): ecedweb.unomaha.edu/k-12/k-5concepts.cfm

Holly Thompson's website: hatbooks.com

ACKNOWLEDGMENTS

Thank you to my editors at Henry Holt, Laura Godwin and Julia Sooy, and to my agent, Jamie Weiss Chilton of the Andrea Brown Literary Agency. Also, a huge shout-out to the many SCBWI Japan members who shared feedback as this novel evolved. Special thanks to my Kamakura readers: Kris Kosaka, Alexander O. Smith, Heather Willson, and my husband, Bob Pomeroy. And deepest thanks, admiration, and hugs to my own children and their friends, and to children everywhere who have attended schools as second-language speakers or outsiders and have strived to find and make peace.